EXCEPTION TO THE RULE

by Cindy Rizzo

First Edition November 2013

Copyright 2013 Cindy T. Rizzo

Editors: Nikki Busch and Jayne Fereday

Cover Design: Jan Wandrag

For Jennifer

The wonderful exception to every rule

PART I
1993-1994

CHAPTER ONE

Robin Greene looked around her bare dorm room with most of her stuff still packed and piled high. She stood surveying her belongings, her hands in the pockets of her jeans, her short, dark, wavy hair falling onto her forehead and into her eyes. She debated whether to attend the hall meeting, due to start in five minutes, even though she'd rolled her eyes at the girl who stopped by to tell her it would be held in the lounge at four o'clock. While engaging in this kind of group activity was out of step with the anarchistic, cynical image she was hoping to project, it could help her get a grip on her surroundings, something she found herself desperately needing. The truth was she needed to know the lay of the land. In uncertain situations she knew it was better when she could find an exit sign or, at the very least, that place on a map that announced, "you are here." So she figured she could tolerate the hall meeting to check out whether this college thing was as hopeless as it seemed.

Even now, she was still a little stunned that she had let her parents talk her into going to Adams University in the godforsaken suburbs of Boston, instead of staying in New York City where her friends and her real life were based.

"They have a college in the Village, you know," she'd told them.

All summer she'd had to constantly remind herself about the writers who ran the new program to which she'd applied and been accepted. She would now have the opportunity to work closely with incredible novelists, including her literary hero, Joe Donovan, whose books were based in the gritty neighborhoods of Boston and defined her own aspirations for the kind of stories she wanted to tell and the way she wanted to tell them.

3

After seeing an article about the author in the Sunday *Times*, her father had told her that Donovan had recently been a guest of President Bill Clinton's at the White House.

"Seems we have the same taste in books as the President, Robbie," he had said with a wink.

She remembered when Joe himself had called her at home urging her to enroll at Adams and promising her that he would do everything in his power to make sure she could develop her talent and write undisturbed.

But even with these good things on the horizon, she still worried that she'd become just like her mother, who had sacrificed her real desire to remain in the edgy world of New York City for something safer. The funny thing was that right now, the last thing she felt was safe. From what she could tell so far, this picture-perfect campus tucked away outside the city was filled with hundreds of dull, ambitious, straight suburban students, like the ones she had left behind in the suburbs of Long Island. Closing the door to her room as she left for the hall meeting, Robin despaired that in this whole school there was probably no one like her.

When she arrived, the lounge was filled with eager female students sitting on worn couches and the floor, many with anxious looks on their faces. A tall woman with stick straight, long dark hair, a formfitting dark green dress and lots of jewelry stood at the front smiling. Gabriela, or Gabi as she told everyone to call her, was the Resident Advisor, or RA as she told everyone to say. She was from Madrid, an international student she announced proudly, and spent the next five minutes explaining that an international student was a student from another country. *Was this college or kindergarten?* Robin wondered, and were these other girls so stupid that Gabi felt the need to explain the obvious? Or was Gabi just a pompous jerk?

She told the assembled freshmen that she was a senior and was there to help them. She wanted them to come to her because freshman year could be "so scary." She hoped in time they'd become a family.

Robin tuned out and looked around the room. Not many of them stood out to her. *Seen one straight, middle-class girl ...*, she mused. While Gabi droned on, Robin occupied herself by typecasting the women in the room. That one whispering to several people would be the party girl. That other one sitting with her arms wrapped around her knees would live in the library. She seriously doubted that there was anyone with whom she might have anything in common. But as she sat musing, annoyed that she hadn't grabbed a notebook and pen to get this all down, she was stopped by the sight of a striking blonde sitting to her left, closer to the front of the room. She was dressed in tight white jeans that covered impossibly long legs and a bright pink, low-cut, sleeveless blouse that showed off her glowing, tanned face. Robin had to consciously close her gaping mouth. *Wow, was she gorgeous.* She felt her pulse quicken until she heard the blonde speak up in a sickeningly sweet Southern accent.

"Hi y'all. I'm Tracy Patterson, from Durham, North Car'lina and this is my first time up north. As you can imagine, y'all are a little intimidatin' for someone like me. I'm used to a more, well, a slower pace of life. And so I was hopin' if y'all would be kind enough to fill a little Southern girl in on what I can expect from these Northern boys I've heard so much about."

The room broke out into a fit of giggles, which quickly became a raucous discussion about "Northern boys," with Gabi gladly facilitating. Robin felt as if she'd been punched in the stomach. The overwhelming heterosexuality felt thick, like humidity in August. She moved her legs in preparation to leave, wanting to make a point that her departure was connected to this discussion. Then she noticed someone sitting on the other side of the room against the opposite wall. She was pretending to be interested in what was being said, but was tuning out despite her best efforts. Robin wondered what was separating her from the group despite her apparent struggle to be part of things. Catching her eye with a look that said "Can you believe we're stuck in this place?" eyes rolling, head tipped back, the girl flashed a magnetic smile and looked away. Robin kept watching her. She had an interesting face: olive complexion, dark eyes that were inviting and open, and wavy, layered black hair probably just cut for the beginning of school. She was cute, especially when all that warmth poured out through her smile. *Not edgy or hot enough to be my type*, Robin decided, but there was something nonetheless appealing.

Distracted again by the Southerner who kept talking in the same affected way she had begun, Robin was intrigued by something in her tone that she could only describe as inauthentic. There was a forced quality in the blonde's voice as she responded extra kindly and with great deference to the pieces of wisdom being offered to her. Her accent was way over the top, an exaggeration that went beyond stereotype.

"Ahh jus' don't know what Ah would do without y'all to help me through these first few weeks."

Glancing over at the dark-haired girl, Robin read her reactions. Like everyone, she had been amused at the blonde's initial declaration, but yet more reserved. Then her brown eyes were elsewhere, her mind out of that room, during the horrid straight girl discussion. For the first time since the meeting began, Robin actually smiled as she thought, *Hmmmm, spaces out when the subject turns to guys.*

A few minutes later, Gabi announced that they had gotten off to a great, fun start, and that her door was always open, except of course when her boyfriend, Philip, was visiting. At once, they all stood up to leave, small clusters of conversation forming among them. Determined to catch up with the dark-haired girl, Robin positioned herself right outside the door

6

and waited. As they came face-to-face, she summoned her courage and leaned over to speak into the girl's ear.

"Well this was thrilling, wasn't it?"

Confused for a second, the girl offered another incredible smile, a chuckle, and the nod of her head.

"I'm forcing myself to keep an open mind," she said, cheering Robin with a much-needed confirmation of their shared view. "Hi," she continued, extending her hand in greeting, "I'm Angie."

Robin looked at the waiting hand, thinking the gesture hokey and feeling self-conscious. She squeezed Angie's fingers lightly, letting go immediately.

"Robin." Her voice was almost a whisper. Her cheeks felt warm as she said her own name aloud.

They walked down the hall together in an unspoken effort to move away from their hall mates.

"Which is your room?" Angie asked.

"Uh, 438." Robin pointed down the hall to the left.

She was rewarded with the smile. "440. We're neighbors!" Angie stopped walking and put her hand on Robin's arm. "How's your roommate?"

Robin shrugged. "Don't know, haven't met her yet. If I'm lucky, she won't show."

Up until meeting Angie, Robin had been planning to develop a reputation as an eccentric recluse, the perfect cover so she could be left alone. Now she wondered instead if she had found someone she could talk to.

Angie sighed. "Mine's a cheerleader type who put pictures of her boyfriend up all over the room,"

Robin was surprised to hear this cheerful woman speak negatively about anything.

"The Southern belle?" Robin asked, wondering if Angie had really lost the roommate lottery.

"Nooooo," Angie grinned and leaned over to Robin in an attempt to not be overheard. "Wasn't she a trip? So affected. Like something straight out of Tennessee Williams."

"Yeah," Robin said nodding her head, "though I'm wondering if *straight* is the operable word."

Angie's eyes were a question waiting to be answered. Closely the smile returned, more brilliant now than before.

"Do you want to go down to dinner together later?" she asked.

CHAPTER TWO

In addition to functioning as her cover, Brett had always been Tracy's connection to reality. His clear, deep drawl, blue eyes, and reassuring smile kept her sane all through high school. She was desperate to be with him at Duke where, if nothing else, she knew how people thought and acted. But her father had begged her, bribed her and convinced her to go to Adams, where he had gotten both his undergrad and medical degrees. She had agreed, but with the condition that he not push her about going pre-med. She dreaded the thought of taking all those chemistry and biology courses. While she was eager to study psychology, she had no intention of becoming a psychiatrist like him.

At the time she made her decision to attend school in Boston, it had felt like it could be the beginning of a big adventure. New city, new start; far from home and all the constraints she'd had to manage. But now that she was here, she was disoriented by the fact that the North felt like another country. Everyone rushed around with their heads down, rudely pushed you aside and stared when you said, "Good morning."

She opened the large red suitcase that held all the heavy clothes she'd bought in anticipation of a frightful winter. Oh, why wasn't she with Brett right now, instead of here in this awful place where it would soon be freezing and would never stop snowing? Her long blonde hair was tied back and her white jeans and pink blouse clung to her in the hot, humid weather. God, didn't they believe in air conditioning up here?

She felt imprisoned by these foreign surroundings and realized that the only way she could feel safe was to construct the false persona she had debuted at the hall meeting. *Might as well put on a good show*, she reasoned. *This is what they think I am anyway—a Southern Belle, boy crazy, a little ditzy, and unschooled in big city ways. At least if I act the part I can get the protection these lies offer.* Besides, she concluded, in Brett's absence they felt like a necessity.

In this unfamiliar place, there'd be no handsome track star to rescue her, no pretend boyfriend to provide a cover for what she was really after. Oh, it's possible she could seek out some other good looking, gay, all-American male who needed the same kind of façade she did, but something made her hesitate to do so. She had been hoping for college to provide a new way to deal with life, but so far she couldn't see one. When she thought about the months ahead, all she could picture in her head was this abandoned road that rose up and suddenly ended.

As she stared into the last empty suitcase she had just unpacked, looking around for an out-of-the-way place to store it, she thought, *I guess I'll have to make the best of Daddy's precious alma mater. And I'll begin by learning how to deal with these Northern girls. These Yankees can't be too hard to figure out.*

She surveyed the depressing dorm room with its cinderblock walls painted a dingy beige and resolved to at least make her own space look more like home. She could put curtains on the window, repaint using a sunnier color and decorate with pictures of Chapel Hill and Hilton Head beach, anything to make the place feel warmer. Her roommate had arrived a day late, dumped her things on her side of the room and told Tracy she needed to untangle a mess with the Registrar's Office and would be back later.

Exhausted from unpacking and the heat, Tracy lay on her yellow bedspread and thought back to that last weekend on the beach at Hilton Head wondering if she could recreate a similar arrangement up here at school.

#

The late August sun baked the smooth white sand of the Hilton Head beach where Tracy laid her towel. She sat up, putting more suntan

10

lotion on the exposed part of her middle that wasn't covered by the red striped bikini. When she lay back down, the warmth radiating up from the sand soothed and relaxed her back.

She'd gotten out of bed early without waking Millicent, so she could catch some morning rays in the quiet solitude. This was her last full day here and she was hoping to make the most of it.

Her hair was tied back for now, but when she turned over she'd loosen it so it would bleach in the sun. It had already turned a few shades lighter, which pleased her because the contrast made her tan even more noticeable.

She closed her eyes and thought back on the summer. It was fun for the most part. She'd snuck away with Millicent to her beach house a few weekends and also spent time with a succession of women she'd met at the bar and at a picnic. There had been no shortage of sex this summer that was for sure. *Might as well get it now*, she reasoned. Who knew what awaited her up north in Boston where she didn't know a soul. Would her looks and charm even work there? For all she knew she was heading into a desert, a very cold and snowy desert.

"So this is where you've gone off to?" Millicent stood in the sand next to where Tracy lay on the towel.

Tracy craned her head up, turning her body slightly to the side to look at Millicent who towered above her in an orange caftan and sandals, her short, light brown hair messy from sleep.

"Hey, you," she said, smiling. "I thought I'd get a jump start on my last full day here."

"Hmm," Millicent said, her eyes wide. "I was hopin' for a little bit of a different jump start with you."

Tracy pushed herself up onto her forearms and smiled. "I'm sure that could be arranged," she said, getting to her feet.

11

Millicent Farrell was the president of the local garden club and former head of the Durham Junior League, which for some reason made her a very important person in town. A woman in her early forties, with a son away at college and a husband who conveniently made himself scarce, Millicent used her cover of unimpeachable respectability to indulge her taste in beautiful, younger women like Tracy Patterson.

Tracy knew she was just the latest of Millicent's little trophy girls, but it made no difference to her because she regarded Millicent as just another of her own conquests. She'd already lasted longer than the previous young lovers, because Millicent knew she wanted nothing more than the beach in summer, a warm fireplace in the winter, and a lot of sex.

"You're like me, Tracy," Millicent once said. "You don't go in for all that love stuff, do you?"

Tracy shrugged. "Guess not." She had realized very quickly that the less she said to Millicent, the better. After all, she was her mother's best friend.

Tracy had been able to construct a life at home that let her have all the fun she wanted with women, while at the same time keeping her safe from the judgments of her parents, friends, and everyone else. She saw no advantage in analyzing her interest in older women. These attractions had begun the summer after she turned fifteen, when she'd seduced a camp counselor, and continued a year later with a dance instructor and then the obligatory gym teacher. There were also the women in the bars: older, more butch, and very hot. It all came pretty easily when you had classic feminine good looks—silky, blonde hair; soft, green eyes; and long, firm dancer's legs.

Yes, there'd been a few boys. But Tracy never liked the feel of their bodies or the way their lips felt on hers. She figured out pretty quickly that it wasn't the fault of the individual boys she'd dated; it was just that she only wanted to be with women.

She followed Millicent up the gradual incline toward the house and stopped next to the outdoor shower.

"I've gotta wash off the sand and the lotion. Why don't you join me?" Tracy said, pulling Millicent by the hand as she turned on the shower.

Millicent stood beyond the reach of the spray.

"I don't need a shower," she said in what Tracy had come to think of as her mother voice.

Tugging at Millicent's hand, Tracy looked directly into the woman's gray-blue eyes.

"If you get in here with me, I'm sure to figure out something you do need," she said with an inviting smile.

Millicent took a quick look around up and down the beach and, seeing no one, lifted the caftan over her head, slipped off her sandals and let the warm water fall onto her back and shoulders before fully immersing her head.

Facing Millicent, Tracy reached up to tilt the taller woman's head down a bit and kissed her, stepping in close. Millicent pulled Tracy to her, deepening the kiss and moving her hands first down Tracy's arms and then her back, finally landing on her bottom. She used that vantage point to pull the lower parts of their bodies together, positioning Tracy's leg between hers as she began to move on it.

Tracy moaned and lowered her head to taste Millicent's breasts, lapping the shower water that dripped down to her now hardened, brown nipples. Tracy sucked and gently bit one nipple and then the other. She moved a free hand over Millicent's belly and then lower to the place between her legs. Millicent moved her body against Tracy's hand, still holding fast to the firm bottom and squeezing it toward her.

"Yesss," the older woman called out over the sound of the water. "Don't stop what you're doing. Ohhh, yes."

Tracy was dizzy with the intensity of what was happening. Being out in the morning sun with the water enveloping them; Millicent's hands grabbing her bottom as she took Tracy's puckered, hard nipple into her mouth; and her insistent movement against Tracy's hand, bathed in a different kind of wetness, appearing and then instantly washing away.

As she came close to her peak and release, Millicent braced her left arm against the shower stall and screamed a loud, "Ohhh. Ohhh." as the spasms radiated up from between her legs.

When they had subsided, she released Tracy and took a half step back, not yet able to focus.

Tracy smiled at her and reached outside the spray for one of the dry towels that were stored in a recess on the side wall, safely away from the water.

"Here," she said as she handed the towel to Millicent. "Now I'd really like to take my shower. I'll meet you up in the house in a few minutes."

Soon after, when Tracy slid the glass rear door open to enter the house, Millicent was on the phone listening to someone talking. She raised a finger to her lips signaling Tracy to be quiet. Wrapped only in a towel, holding her wet bikini, Tracy headed for the bedroom as she heard Millicent's mother voice again, this time responding angrily to her son, Bradley Jr.

"Junior, I am telling you that this girl is not for you!"

Pause.

"No, I don't need to meet her. You need to break this off right now. This is not the life your father and I want for you."

Pause.

14

"You say that now, but mark my words, her background will catch up with her in time and it'll ruin you."

Pause.

"Junior? Junior? Oh damn."

She slammed the phone back in place on the wall and headed for the bedroom.

"Hang up on me, will you?" Millicent said aloud to herself as she walked toward Tracy.

Pulling a lilac V-necked t-shirt over her head, Tracy turned toward Millicent with a questioning look.

"Some girl he met up at that school in Philadelphia. Irish and Catholic. Father runs a messenger service. Her father is a messenger, for godsakes!"

"And what's wrong with that?" Tracy asked, departing from her usual practice of not engaging in these kinds of pointless conversations with Millicent.

"You are joking, right Tracy? Poor, Catholic, from the North? What is right with that is the better question? I give it six months at best."

Millicent sat on the bed still wrapped in a towel, her head bent forward resting in her hands. All at once, she stood up and turned to face Tracy, a delighted smile forming on her face.

"Tracy? You know, you would be a wonderful match for Junior. You're just the kind of girl he needs. You have the looks, the breeding, the poise."

The rush of words spilled out of her.

"I mean, of course, you'd go off to college, but in a few years, you two could be married and raising a family back in Durham."

Tracy stood frozen in place staring openmouthed at Millicent. Her only impulse was to laugh in response, but she knew that once she started the pure absurdity of Millicent's little fantasy would make her unable to stop. She closed her mouth tightly, pressing her lips together, and literally biting her tongue, still staring as she fought for composure. At last she responded in a quiet, careful voice.

"Millicent, I'm not quite sure that would be a fair thing to do to Bradley."

Millicent looked confused.

"Why on earth not?"

Tracy could not imagine being in a more ludicrous conversation.

"You have to ask that?"

"Oh, Tracy," Millicent said, coming toward her. "At some point, you have to make a real life for yourself."

She pulled Tracy close.

"This ..." She placed a quick kiss on Tracy's lips. "... is not a way to live respectably. You know that."

Tracy knew this was a losing battle and that some version of anything she said to challenge Millicent could get back to her mother. Besides, she hadn't yet figured out if there wasn't a grain of truth in what Millicent was saying. It wasn't that she was ashamed of who she was, but she had no sense of how it could translate into an adult life. She wanted a career and a family and, yes, she wanted some form of respectability, not likely the same brand as Millicent's, but she wasn't sure she was that comfortable being resigned to living as an outcast.

Could two women together make a life in a place like Durham? She didn't think it would be possible and she had no desire to try such a crazy idea. It was all very confusing. When she tried to imagine her life even as soon as next month, she could only picture a road that slanted up like the beginning of a long bridge going over the causeway and then suddenly ended without warning. There's the climb, the road, and then nothing. She

16

resolved in that moment to enjoy these last few hours of the life she knew well, and not to think past today.

As she pulled up her white shorts and buttoned them in place, she at last looked at Millicent and said in a quiet voice, "What I'd really like to do today is go shopping."

CHAPTER THREE

Robin began the task of unpacking, beginning with the things she cared most about—her books, her writing journals, her CDs, and her stereo. She dug deep into one of the duffels for her leather jacket, and when she unfolded it, she found a book nestled inside with a bright yellow post-it note attached to the cover.

"Dear Robbie." She recognized her mother's loopy script immediately. "As writers have inspired my art, may your writing be inspired by the work of artists. Love, Mom."

The book was titled "Mapplethorpe" and on the cover was a large black and white photo of one of the artist's eyes, open and penetrating. Robin sat on the still bare mattress of her bed and leafed through the book, thrilled to find the photo of Mapplethorpe in his leather jacket inside. This was the same photo that she had hanging up in her room at home—a self-portrait of the artist with a shock of dark hair hanging over his forehead. This very image had been her inspiration for the purchase of the beat-up, black leather jacket she had bought in the East Village last March. She smiled as she remembered her mother's reaction when she'd brought the jacket home.

"This is all you got with the hundred dollars I gave you?" Wendy Greene exclaimed.

Robin reacted predictably, rolling her eyes and retorting.

"Are you afraid I'm buying cocaine or heroin with the money?"

Her mother shook her head, smiling. She sighed, exhaling. "Let me see how it fits."

Robin pushed her fists through the limp sleeves and grabbed both sides of the zipper-edged opening on top as if it was a suit jacket with

18

lapels. The jacket, likely worn before by an adult male, reached a little past her hips, but her broad shoulders fit it well. She put her lips together in a scowl and looked intently at her mother to maximize the effect of her charcoal-colored eyes. Then she smiled.

"I'm going for a Mapplethorpe look," she said.

Wendy nodded appreciatively.

"I see it," she said without a hint of sarcasm in her voice.

As Robin held the large photo book to her chest and thought about her mother, the usual conflicted thoughts surfaced. She got up and put the book on her empty desk and then rifled through a dented cardboard box looking for the new sheet set and blanket her mother had bought from Macy's. Thinking, *this bed isn't going to make itself*, she set about unfolding the crisp, light blue and white striped sheets, all the while recalling her last night at home. Her mother had once again tried to justify and explain her life and the choices she'd made.

"Robbie, you know I never intended to live in this wasteland called suburbia," she said, almost pleading, "but I inherited this house and we wanted you and your brother to go to good schools."

Her body sagged in sad resignation as she fell back into the cushions of the navy blue armchair in their living room. Her short, stocky frame (which Robin viewed as her own unlucky inheritance), was too uncomfortable to remain upright. Pushing a strand of straight, light brown hair away from her eyes and off her forehead, her mother continued, talking as much to herself as to Robin.

"I wanted to move to the country. You know, the whole back to the land thing. Oh Robbie, you could have been one of those plump little children who ran around naked in large green fields or who rolled down steep hills like it was nothing. I wanted you to have that sense of freedom, of few limits."

Robin watched her mother intently, still struck by the similarity of their bodies, but almost relieved that she was darker in coloring and had angular features, like her father. Feelings of helplessness and pity filled Robin's stomach and she had to look away from her mother's sunken form. In that moment Robin saw that Wendy Greene had punished herself way more than a moody, queer daughter who spent too much money on a leather jacket ever could. She mumbled something to her mother about it being okay and that she had to leave to meet her friends in the city. Wendy smiled and slowly raised her body up from the chair.

"All right then, sweetie. Be careful and have a good time." her parting words.

"I can't do both, Mom," Robin said.

They laughed together, relieved at the change in mood, and Robin left the house for her final night with her friends in the West Village.

#

As the Long Island Rail Road entered the tunnel for the last leg of the journey into Manhattan, Robin reasoned that there would be plenty of time tomorrow to be sullen, to complain about the long drive to Boston, and to dread the prospect of boring classes. But tonight was her last night to feel alive.

She sprinted off the train as soon as the doors whooshed open and bounded up the stairs through the noise and grime of Penn Station, grabbing the number 1 train downtown to the Village. She met Sophia and TJ at their usual place in Sheridan Square, along with two new kids they'd brought with them from the homeless youth shelter. Upon Robin's arrival, they pooled their money. Robin threw two twenty-dollar bills into the pile that rested in TJ's large, cupped hands.

"Whoa ho, Greene, moneybags," TJ cried out closing her hands together to hold onto the bills and coins. "College girl's treating tonight!"

They all crowded around Robin at once, clasping her arms and patting her on the back. Their excitement helped to lessen the embarrassment she'd felt when her large contribution had been singled out.

"You can thank my parents for this," she said, pointing her chin at the money in TJ's hands.

One of the new kids moved closer to Robin and pushed up her light blue button down shirt to reveal a dark red welt on her right side. "Yeah?" she said. "And you can thank mine for this."

Everyone gasped. Robin wanted to fall through the subway grate where she stood and slink all the way back to Long Island.

Sophia's large round body and genuine look of concern closed in on the kid, whose bright red hair competed with the angry red stripe on her side.

"'S'okay, I'm fine" she told Sophia who then backed off.

Sophia turned her attention back to Robin.

"I don't think you should be paying for us, Robbie. We should be treating you tonight. This is your goodbye party."

She walked over and put her hands on Robin's shoulders.

Sophia and Robin had had a short-lived fling awhile back, but they soon silently slid into a friendship by mutual agreement. All of them had been sexual with one another at some point just for the hell of it, though none of them did relationships. Why bother, when sex was so plentiful and uncomplicated?

Looking at Sophia and then Robin, TJ pushed the bills and coins into the front pocket of her worn black jeans. At almost six feet with a wide girth, TJ was the tallest and largest member of the group. It was safest then that she be the one to carry the money.

"I tell you what," TJ said, raising a finger so they'd all listen. "I'll make you a deal, Greene. We spend your money and in exchange, I'll find a girl for you tonight who'll give you a personal send-off. Whaddya think?"

Robin had been looking down at the ground during the conversation about money and parents. Her short, stocky frame was bent slightly forward and her wavy, dark hair was in her eyes. But TJ's bargain got her spirits up. She lifted her head to face each member of her little group.

"Sounds good," she said, grinning.

They walked down Christopher Street toward the pier to check out who was around and to score a joint with some of the money they had. TJ bought one from a trans woman she knew and they stood close together passing it around. When they finished, TJ broke away while the others stood against a railing, surveying the crowd of kids cast in shadow in the twilight.

Ten minutes later, TJ returned accompanied by two people they didn't know. One was a white girl with long, light brown hair and gorgeous, tapered legs. Robin looked at her and gulped, her palms sweaty. *Princess alert*, she thought. *Stay away. If I'd wanted Long Island I would have stayed there.* The other girl was a cute, pudgy, light-skinned, black girl with cornrows and glasses. Robin smiled at her and TJ took notice.

"Olivia, meet Robbie. Tonight is Robbie's big send-off. Our pal's going up the river for a bit." TJ turned toward the Hudson pointing north. "So we wanted to make this a special night."

Robin looked at TJ and then at Olivia moving closer to her.

"It's not what you think," she said. "I'm going to Boston. For school."

"Oh wow." Olivia exhaled and they began to walk together away from the group.

As they made their way toward the end of the pier, Robin started her usual routine, half seduction ploy and half writer in search of a story. She usually asked one or two initial questions to get all the kids like Olivia to open up and then she just listened with very little additional prompting. Most embellished their exploits on the street, especially their sexual adventures. But they never exaggerated what put them there in the first place—neglectful, abusive parents; a string of horror stories based in a series of foster homes; and the church, always the church. That had been TJ's downfall. Her uncle was some big shot in the Greek Orthodox Church and Theodora Jaclyn's large, butch presence and interest in the cute teenage girls at St. Helena's was enough to get her thrown out of her parents' house.

Occasionally, there was one like Robin and probably the brown-haired girl TJ had brought over as an offering, who were just there to escape the stifling conformity of the suburbs.

Olivia was in the other category. Although she still lived in the Bronx with her mother, her aunt, and her older brother, she was checking out the pier to decide whether she should leave home. Her problem was her brother, whom she described as "a crazy MF who won't leave me alone." Robin recognized the code words for sexual abuse, another common issue she heard about a lot on the pier.

As they stood together looking over the Hudson and the shoreline of New Jersey, Olivia took Robin's hand and gave her a kiss on the cheek. Robin smiled at her and winked, her head tilted to the left.

Olivia stepped closer and whispered, "Any place we can go to be alone?"

Robin nodded and walked her back toward her friends.

An hour later TJ stood guard in front of a bathroom at The Well, a nearby bar that didn't look too closely at fake IDs. Robin's contribution to

23

the night's pool of cash had bought them all many shots of tequila and whiskey and, after a particularly intense slow dance during which Olivia pushed Robin's hand down between her legs, she guided Olivia into the bathroom knowing that TJ would see to it that they weren't interrupted.

Robin backed Olivia up against the white tiled wall of the small grungy room, her mouth fixed on the slightly shorter girl's, their tongues exploring. She reached under Olivia's bright pink tank top and felt a soft, fleshy stomach. Olivia moaned at the touch and Robin whispered in her ear.

"You want this?

"Oh yes," Olivia said.

Robin removed the girl's glasses, reaching over with one hand to place them carefully on the closed toilet seat. With all systems a go, Robin moved back under the tank top and up to Olivia's bra, feeling the soft and ample breasts underneath, finding the hardening nipples through the fabric. She reached behind and opened the bra in one practiced motion, lifting Olivia's shirt along with the bra toward her head.

"You're sure it's okay to do this here?" Olivia asked.

Robin continued until the shirt and bra were all the way off and looked directly into Olivia's dark brown eyes.

"No one's gonna mess with the six-foot, 300-pound butch at the door. Don't worry."

Reassured, Olivia moved closer, kissing with her tongue deep inside Robin's mouth. Robin reached down and unbuttoned Olivia's black shorts, tugging at the zipper. Olivia moved her hips forward and back and the shorts dropped to her ankles.

Robin bent her head down to take first one and then the other large breast into her mouth. She loved the feeling of a hardening nipple as she teased it with her tongue and teeth. Olivia groaned and Robin made sure

24

the girl's back was supported by the bathroom wall so she could release one hand from Olivia's hips and reach down into her underwear.

As she found the silky place between Olivia's legs, Robin remembered the girl's brother, moved her hand away a little and spoke softly into Olivia's ear.

"We can stop at any time. Give me a word, any word, and when you say it, I'll take my hand away and back off. What's the word?" she asked.

Olivia looked a little confused, her eyes unfocused. She turned her head to the right and then back to Robin.

"Faucet," she said.

Robin smiled at her. "Okay, faucet it is." Olivia smiled back.

They kissed for a minute. Robin moved her hand back to the hardened nipples and then returned to where she had been before. Olivia was wet and ready, which boosted Robin's confidence and put her concerns to rest. She entered Olivia and began moving her fingers in a slight rocking motion, in and out. Olivia exhaled forcefully and grabbed Robin's shoulders.

Robin spoke into her ear as she moved her fingers to the swollen flesh of Olivia's clit. "You gonna give me what I want, sweet girl?"

Olivia began to shake and pant, moaning. With her other hand, Robin tightened her grip on the girl's waist as Olivia threw back her head and called out a very loud, "Ohhh God," through the release.

Robin removed her hand from between Olivia's legs and grasped the girl's shoulders at the same time that she positioned Olivia's leg between hers. She was so excited by her own success in getting Olivia off that it only took about a minute of moving against the leg that she clung to in order to find her own satisfaction, even through her jeans.

"You didn't want me to ... touch you?" Olivia said.

"Not necessary, I get what I need from touching and watching you."

25

Olivia began to dress, pulling up the shorts that lay on the floor at her feet and looking for her bra and tank top. Robin carefully picked the girl's glasses up and placed them gently on her face.

In a whispered, tentative voice, Olivia asked, "Would you give me your number?"

Robin hesitated. This was always the awkward moment she had to finesse, but in this instance she had already thought of a response.

"I have no number 'til I get to Boston and figure things out," she said. "Why don't you give me yours?"

Robin pulled out a 3x7 spiral notebook she kept in her jacket pocket with a pen jammed into the wire binding. She opened to the last page, making sure no other girl's number was there and gave it to Olivia.

While Olivia wrote down her number she asked, "Is this your little black book?"

Robin chuckled. "Not really, but it never hurts to have a pen and paper when you need it."

What she didn't say is that this was her walking around journal that she used to record observations and stories about her life in the city. Olivia never saw the first half of the book that was filled with accounts of Robin's time at the pier and her sexual escapades and musings on the taste and feel of the West Village. Worried that her friends would think she was some kind of reporter slumming for a story, Robin never told any of them about her writing. She needed to protect her place among them so she would always have an escape from the suburbs. The writing was merely the thing she did without thinking, kind of like breathing.

After one final hug, Robin led Olivia out of the bathroom. TJ nodded and stepped away from guarding the door.

"Hey, sweet girl," Robin said, looking at Olivia. "I gotta get going. TJ here is gonna go on a little walk with me. Take care of yourself, okay? And remember," Robin said, smiling, "use the *faucet* when you need to."

Olivia blushed and looked down at the floor. Robin motioned TJ over.

"Walk me to the train for old times' sake?"

"Only because it's your last night."

After saying goodbye to the others, hugging Sophia through her friend's tears, Robin and TJ headed out of the bar toward the Christopher Street station.

"Teej, I need you to do me a favor."

"I thought I already did that tonight."

"Yeah, but I need another one."

"What the fuck now? You're wearing out your goodbye, Greene."

Robin smiled and took the notebook out of her pocket, tearing out the last page with Olivia's number.

"Call that little girl Olivia from the bar ..."

"What? You're pawning her off on me?"

"Hold on. She's got a pervert brother who can't keep his thing in his pants. I want you to show her those moves that you taught me so she can get away from him in case he comes looking for her."

TJ had taught Robin how to defend herself against the drunken assholes who populated the Long Island Rail Road late at night. Her moves had come in handy once or twice.

"What am I, social services, for God's sakes?" said TJ. "I should get paid for this shit."

Robin knew despite this show of bravado that TJ would make the call and help Olivia.

"Your payback is the good karma you'll get when you come back reincarnated as a chicken and no one can catch you for dinner," Robin grinned and began running a little ahead of TJ to get beyond her reach.

"Who ya callin' chicken, you little pipsqueak?"

TJ quickly caught up to Robin. "Besides, karma don't put money in my pocket, you know."

As they reached the entrance to the subway, Robin looked up at TJ and said, "I guess this is goodbye, huh?"

"You'd better do some damage up there in Boston with all those college girls. I'm counting on you Greene." She wagged her finger at Robin. "And remember our pact, no princesses."

Robin nodded and smiled at her friend.

"See ya Teej."

Robin wrapped her arms around TJ's middle, not quite able to reach all the way around. TJ grabbed Robin under her arms and lifted her off the ground.

"Thanks for everything," Robin said into TJ's shoulder, her tears threatening. "You're a great pal. Stay safe."

"Yeah, go get smart up in that school," TJ said in a shaky voice. "But not too smart, you hear?"

Back on solid ground, Robin turned and headed down the stairs to catch the train to Penn Station. It was hard to see the turnstile through her tears. As she waited for the train, she wiped her eyes with the side of her hand.

Once the headlights of the 1 train came into view in the tunnel and began to grow larger, Robin got ready for the long ride back to Long Island. Turning her thoughts to the day ahead of her and to the unknown life she'd soon be living, she wondered, *What now?*

CHAPTER FOUR

When Robin and Angie snaked through the ridiculously long food line and set their trays down at a vacant table, Robin fired off the only question she had thought worth asking.

"So what's the deal here? Are you a lesbian?"

Shocked at Robin's directness and at the almost accusatory nature of the question, Angie grabbed the edge of the table, her eyes wide. Robin stared at her, chin jutting out, head tilted to the left. She watched as Angie calmed herself, releasing the table from her grasp, looking Robin straight in the eyes, defiant, yet even now strangely pleasant.

"Yes." Angie's voice was calm, a witness in the box with nothing to hide. "And I assume you are too?"

Good come back, Robin thought, smiling. "Uh huh," was her short confirmation.

Well, then, Angie wanted to know everything. Robin started to feel like a contestant on a lesbian quiz show.

With elbows on the table and her head resting on her folded hands, Angie's interrogation began. "What was your coming out like?"

Robin sat back in her chair, arms crossed, with an amused smile on her face. "Uneventful. I always knew I liked girls and not boys"

"Do your parents know?"

"Yes. They're hipper than I am. My mother said she knew I didn't like boys and was relieved that I'd one day have some kind of intimate relationship. My dad told me not to miss the Gay Pride Parade in New York City."

"Have you had many girlfriends?"

"I don't do girlfriends, just friends and sex."

"Have you read the new books by Audre Lorde and Jane Rule?"

"Yes, Audre Lorde is brilliant. Who's Jane Rule?"

"Have you ever seen Sweet Honey in the Rock in concert?"

"No, most of my friends are homeless and have no money for concerts."

And finally, "Which Indigo Girl do you think is cuter?"

"Emily. And she's the better writer." To which Angie replied, "you have no taste in women."

Robin found herself recounting her adventures in the Village. She talked about the girls she had met and the trans guys and gay men, how the easy flow of sexual energy turned friends into lovers and then back into friends. She was deliberately explicit with Angie, talking about "fucking girls" and "coming again and again." She described shuttling on the Long Island Rail Road, sometimes at three in the morning, eager to leave the place she called "my parents' house" for the city where she could just be. And she told Angie about her friends and how they'd been kicked out of their homes or had run away to escape endless abuse, preferring to try their luck on the streets.

As she listened, Angie settled down from her initial "oh, wow" reaction to a more contemplative and quiet nodding of her head. In fact, Robin realized that although Angie had offered little commentary on these intentionally shocking and amusing stories, she was actually a critical listener. Her smiles were a kind of road map of her reactions. The big, wide ones signaled appreciation or excitement, and Robin had to give her credit, she'd delivered up some of those throughout all of the sex stories. The more closemouthed smiles indicated that Angie didn't quite believe all of what she was hearing. And then the medium-sized smiles, mouth partly open, head nodding, meant she was following closely, wanting to hear more. *She's smart*, Robin thought to herself, *a little enthusiastic for my tastes, but I like her.*

She hadn't expected to make a connection with someone so quickly, especially someone she wasn't hot for. But Angie was interesting. She told Robin about her family, and how they were all involved in politics. Robin said that couldn't imagine such a family, so Angie explained that public service had always been synonymous with the Antonellis, even before she was born. She mentioned that the high point of her year had been the family's attendance at Bill Clinton's inaugural last January.

"The first Democratic president since I was a baby," she said with great pride.

Angie explained that in her family you were expected to follow your parents into the political world in the same way that you'd be expected to step up and take over if, for example, your family owned a hardware store. Robin just rolled her eyes and shook her head.

Later that night, alone in her dorm room, her roommate still missing in action, Robin stared up at the ceiling as images of smarmy, blow-dried men in suits floated through her mind. She pictured them smiling and greeting voters as they stood behind a store counter ringing up boxes of nails and screws. She picked up the notebook on the floor next to her bed and began to scribble a description of this scene, excited that her rendition of politicians in a hardware store, recorded in pitch dark, was likely being scrawled outside the notebook's thin blue lines, past the straight red margins, probably with words piled on top of one another—visual and written versions of her idea of chaos and incongruity.

This silly burst of creativity had used up the last bit of energy Robin had for the crazy first full day of college that had blessedly come to an end. As she rolled over to go to sleep, she wondered briefly about her mystery roommate, annoyed to be left dangling, but jazzed at the prospect of having the room to herself. Her last thoughts were once again of Angie, who had talked about her attraction to jocks. She confessed that the sight of women playing sports was an instant turn on for her and she would fall for the most obnoxious, ignorant woman if she looked good with a ball in her hands. Athletes, she'd explained, were her "Achilles' heel."

"More like Achilles' hell," Robin had responded.

"Well, we each have our own versions of heaven and hell," Angie had replied.

Angie then launched into the story of her somewhat ambivalent relationship with a soccer player in high school, who was now kicking a ball across a field at Boston College. Robin could only guess at Angie's heaven and hell in that relationship.

But as the darkness surrounding her finally seeped inside her head, slowly blocking all conscious thought, she wondered about and was puzzled by this strange addiction for perfect Angie, the lesbian scion of a Massachusetts political family.

#

Classes for the most part were dull. Robin coasted in her usual way through Sociology 101 (dreadfully stupid) and History 101, which supposedly covered 18th and 19th century European history. She'd overheard a sophomore telling a freshman on her hall that the course was known as "The Sun Never Sets on 101," a reference to the fact that Professor Marsh, an unabashed Anglophile, concentrated solely on the glory years of the British Empire, ignoring entirely all of the countries of continental Europe. Marsh, who was right out of central casting, actually wore tweed jackets with suede elbow patches and spoke with an affected British accent. *He's probably from the Bronx*, Robin thought.

The semester's saving graces, besides Angie, were Robin's freshman creative writing seminar and Psych 101, presided over by the captivating

Professor Patricia Coolidge. Professor Coolidge entranced some two hundred freshmen three times each week with fifty minutes of lecturing about things that actually mattered. She talked about gender differences, about sex, and about the motivation of the human mind, all things Robin wanted to write about. She told fascinating tales of experiments in which subjects were pushed beyond their usual limits by figures of authority, who urged them to administer painful electric shocks to unsuspecting victims.

"Our willingness to harm the innocent under the guise of following orders is, I submit to you, a flaw so profound it has been responsible for mass genocide, for political upheavals, and maybe even for the continuation of war itself," Professor Coolidge had lectured. "But where then do we go with the findings from Doctor Milgram's experiments? Do we conclude that this defect is such an inevitable part of the fabric of our being that we are helpless to change it? Is the only recourse then to remain vigilant through the ages, guarding against falling victim to this trait in others and in ourselves? Orrrrrr ... "

And here she paused, and walked purposefully away from the lectern toward the first row of students, her unamplified voice rising on its own.

"Is there something about our society, about how we pass on values from one generation to the next, that is actually within our power to change? And thus, are we then ultimately responsible for our actions?

"These questions, ladies and gentlemen, have preoccupied not just pointy-headed academics like myself who sit high up in our ivory towers devising ways of making college students' lives a living hell ... "

There was laughter and a bit of applause.

"No, these questions form the basis of what we have all come to characterize, in our American sound-bite culture, as nature versus nurture. And in handing this dilemma over to you, I am acting as your modern day Rod Serling (any of you know him?)," she asked this rhetorically, which was

33

her usual practice when making reference to old television shows, movies, or rock and roll songs, "in welcoming you to the Twilight Zone of psychology."

She smiled broadly, like someone who knows a secret she's not yet willing to let you in on. Now back at the lectern, her tone downshifted from one of soaring excitement to one of mundane business. Her body, once expressive with gestures and broad movements, was now taut and narrow.

She always wore slacks and a jacket, clothes that gave her stature and authority. Today her above-shoulder length, medium brown hair was worn loose; sometimes she wore it back. She had a perfectly straight nose and large, playful eyes. Angie, who'd once gone up to ask a question after class, reported back that they were a kind of greenish blue. Robin had winced when she actually used the word dreamy.

Now Professor Coolidge was giving her signal that class was ending.

"To help you slog through the treacherous swamp of nature versus nurture," she said in a clipped cadence, "your able teaching assistants will expect you to come to your small group sessions with chapter four of our text under your belts, along with the accompanying reserve reading. Goodbye for now."

Even after her usual sign off, Robin and Angie never got up to leave right away. Instead they watched Professor Coolidge gather her notes and speak to the few students who came up to ask her questions, before she walked out the side entrance at the front of the lecture hall. They were thrilled whenever she took notice of them, flashing a quick smile in their direction as she turned to leave.

Robin tried not to get hooked on these WASP princess types, with their soft straight hair, smooth complexions, and flirty smiles. She'd run into a few in the city and had watched as they circled their prey, drew it in,

34

and then smashed its heart. *No thank you, not for me*, she had concluded after watching one of them work her devious magic on TJ. These types were bad news, especially for susceptible, short and squat, dark-haired Jewish girls from Long Island. Instead, she'd turned her attentions and desires to rebellious baby dykes with Italian, Latin, or Irish surnames, or with African-inspired first names like Takeisha and Asanti. Queers with an edge, just like her.

But, she had to admit, she was as hopeless as Angie with her jock thing, because when these picture-perfect, American Pie girls actually had a brain she found them hard to resist. And this one, who unraveled the mysteries of the universe three times a week, not only had the hair, the skin, and the smile, she had a mega-brain.

"She's gorgeous, absolutely gorgeous," Angie would say after each class, like it was a mantra.

The rumor going around was that Coolidge was a lesbian. Someone had visited her office and had seen pictures on her desk of her with another woman, presumably a partner. With that information, Angie and Robin had become die-hard fans of the psychology professor. One homophobic remark out of anyone, and they would have gladly gone into battle, laying down their lives like two modern day Joans of Arc.

"Hey, I thought you only liked jocks?" Robin said, trying to nudge Angie away from that dead-end obsession.

"And what about you?" Angie said as she pulled the strap of her backpack over her shoulder. "I thought you only liked … What do you like?" she said at last.

Robin threw her head back and laughed. "Hmmm, I think she'd look great in a leather jacket."

Angie reacted with her skeptical smile, shaking her head.

"I think she'd look great in anything … or nothing."

35

They continued to giggle and tease one another as they got up to leave. Robin pointed back over to the front of the lecture hall.

"Have you noticed that the Southern belle from our hall sits right in front every class and waits to leave almost as late as we do?"

"No," said Angie. "During that class, I am watching only one person and you know who that is."

CHAPTER FIVE

Tracy was pacing herself with Professor Coolidge. She was following a tried and true method of slowly increasing the frequency and length of their encounters. First, she made sure the professor noticed her on a regular basis by sitting up front in class. This would serve to build up a sense of curiosity about her. Then she moved in closer with after-class questions, little moments where Tracy's smile and soft skin could be experienced up close. All of this would culminate in the office visit, which usually clinched the deal. The method had never failed with teachers and other adult women back home. There was no reason to think it would now.

Tracy started down the hill from Chandler Hall on her way back to the dorm, still bracing for that first cold snap now that it was early October. The leaves were at their most brilliant yellow, orange, and deep red. *The five minutes on the calendar that is the glory of New England*, she thought dismissively. The Adams campus was pretty standard, with old, red brick buildings around quadrangles and newer glass and stone structures, a basic architectural mish-mash.

Thinking of Patty Coolidge, and how hot she'd looked today in that dark gray jacket, Tracy felt relieved to finally have a focus. She spent a good deal of her alone time planning for and imagining that first time with the professor. The thought of those soft, green-blue eyes and silky brown hair close to her face and body was good for an entire boring freshman English class worth of fantasizing.

When she let herself think about those strong fingers and long legs touching her, she was usually alone in her room, in bed, the pleasure of her thoughts enhanced with the help of her own fingers reaching down to where she was wet and ready. It never took long. She could always finish well within the twenty minutes her roommate spent in the shower.

This time, however, just as she was getting started, the phone rang. Annoyed, she reached over and lifted the receiver slowly, whispering from the bottom of her throat, "Hello."

"Well, hello darlin'. Am I interruptin' something?"

It was Brett, probably the only person she could forgive for this particular interruption.

"Nothing I can't pick up again later," she replied. "How are you, handsome? How are things back home?"

"Just fine, just fine. Still green and warm like summer. How 'bout where you're at? Snowin' pretty hard up there?"

She frowned. This subject was a continuous source of amusement for Brett. He knew this weather thing distressed her and he was relentless in teasing her about it. The thought of all that snow that lay in front of her for months on end brought her back to the grim reality of Boston and the North.

She sighed into the phone. "I miss home."

"You need to start makin' some friends, honey. Now tell me 'bout the girls you been meeting."

So Tracy told Brett about Professor Coolidge and her plans for a hot little affair. Brett listened, joining in with suggestions about how Tracy might reach her goal sooner.

"You know how they are, sweetie. These star professors always want to snag a hot, young student. Just keep doin' what you're doin' and you'll be first in line for your sexy Professor Coolidge."

This was their normal banter. They'd had similar conversations about Tracy's conquests all through high school while each of them functioned as a cover for the other at dances and parties. While everyone

38

thought they were the perfect couple, Tracy was busy sleeping with an ever-changing lineup of older women like Millicent and a host of others.

Brett, on the other hand, had a boyfriend—Jeff Jordan, a football player in their class, who was now also at Duke, having been recruited as an all-state half back. Brett was still running track.

"How's Jeffy?" asked Tracy.

"Oh fine, moody and wonderful as ever. I hardly see him these days, what with practice all the time and his out of town games."

"Are you feeling like you two can be more open about things now that you're at Duke?" Tracy asked.

"Sweet darlin', look at a map; this is still the South. One of us would have to have a sex change operation followed by a skin color change operation for us to feel like we could be more open."

This response disappointed Tracy and brought up all her feelings of sadness for Brett and Jeff and for herself. She had been hoping that getting out of high school in Durham would have been a turning point. Brett and Jeff adored each other and she wanted them to feel good and open about what they had instead of having to hide it all the time.

As she got off the phone, she realized that she was caught in the same trap as her friends, though hers was of her own making. Brett had just as much right to ask when she was going to start being honest about who she really was. Contrary to her original hopes in coming north to Adams, she hadn't made a new start, but instead just relocated all the old stuff from Durham to here, as if it had been packed and unpacked along with her clothing and books. *What's my excuse?* she asked herself. She could think of none. She was just doing what she'd always done to stay safe and to keep her options open. But now it wasn't working. She was lonely and restless to get out of this confined place she had boxed herself into.

I guess it's time to finally take that short walk down the hall. That very long, short walk.

She'd heard some rumors about Angie Antonelli and Robin Greene that intrigued her, although she found Robin's rude and disdainful attitude about everything immature. On the other hand, Angie and she had actually spoken a few times on their way out of the dorm, little friendly exchanges about classes. She liked Angie's warmth and openness. She made an effort to be friendly while other people on their hall were a bit wary of Tracy. Her display at the hall meeting had had the intended effect of creating some distance between her and her neighbors.

The week before, Tracy had been on the periphery of a little cluster of people who were listening to Angie's roommate voice her suspicions that while Angie was nice enough, she had strange tastes in music and books and seemed to have no interest in guys. Her roommate was also horrified that Angie had taken up with Robin. She told the little crowd gathered around her that the two of them were always together, which could only make people talk. Hearing this, Tracy was a little hopeful that maybe there were actually other girls at this school who were like her. It was true that Robin was a bit weird, but at least she could become friends with Angie. At the same time, she worried that making this kind of connection meant she would be taking a step in the direction of giving herself away and she didn't know whether she was entirely ready to do that. But she decided that she could at least investigate the possibility.

Coming up with just the right pretext, Tracy grabbed her psych notebook and headed over to Angie's room. When her knock on the door went unanswered, she took a deep breath and walked two steps toward the next door—Robin's room. They were bound to be hanging out together. Could they possibly be lovers? Tracy hoped not.

She knocked on the door softly, almost tentatively.

40

"Enter," came the reply. It was Robin.

As Tracy stepped inside, the short dark figure glared at her from an armchair in the corner while Angie politely exchanged pleasantries and offered her psychology notes for Tracy's inspection.

Robin's room was just like all their rooms: cinderblock walls painted a dull cream color; flat worn carpeting, a shade darker than the walls; and standard issue beds and desks. The armchair had been carted in from somewhere else, probably the lounge on another floor. Robin had made room for it by moving the empty bed and desk of her non-existent roommate out of the way in a corner.

As Robin's voice drifted over from the far side of the room Tracy looked over.

"So, Tracy, do you *like* Professor Coolidge?" It was more of dare than a question.

After a quick "yes I do," Tracy ignored her and continued to chat with Angie about their classes. Robin remained quiet and sullen, resisting all of Angie's attempts to draw her into the conversation.

Finally, Robin launched another pointed question, this time couched in a mock Southern accent.

"So how are those Northern boys treating you, Tracy?"

They were all at once quiet. Even Angie's usual sense of propriety took a back seat as she waited breathlessly for Tracy's reply.

As Robin's challenge hung in the air, Tracy looked from one to the other, her arms beginning to move in a gesture of response, her mouth half open. And then, like a torrent of late afternoon rain on a stifling summer day, she let loose her reply with characteristic dramatic flair.

"I see my love life here as evolutionary, developing over time as I mature and learn more about life. There is still so much I want to experience in the way of passion. Women have such a blind tendency to

41

just fall in love without thinking. I would rather explore so I can grow into who I am before I make that final choice to love someone with every fiber of my being."

Angie looked both confused by this flowery declaration and interested in hearing more.

"You're full of shit!" Robin shot back as she lay sideways lounging in the armchair, her short legs draped over the side. With a smile of triumph, she continued. "C'mon, let's cut the Blanche Dubois routine and give it up right now. How about you tell us—what does it for you, girls or boys?"

It was clear to Tracy that Robin was a fighter, all scrappy and in your face while Angie's natural inclination was to be the peacemaker and to smooth things over. Angie looked uneasy in response to Robin's direct approach, but she didn't say a word. Instead she stood at the desk gripping the back of her chair, physically restraining herself from voicing some kind of assurance to Tracy that her sexuality was her own business and she didn't have to answer the question. But Tracy realized that Angie's silence also meant that she was as eager as Robin to know the truth. Still, Tracy was angry at having been so rudely provoked and cornered and she was determined to show Robin that she could fight back.

She stood up straight and glared at the figure in the armchair, her body stiff and her eyes narrowed with determination. Robin had been way out of line and Tracy was going to put her in her place. This smart-mouthed New York City girl was not going to get the better of her. She'd see what it was like to tussle with a Southern belle.

"Why, I would venture to say," Tracy began in her exaggerated drawl, "that you already know the answer to that question, because you're such a smart, big city girl. And what chance do I, just a little ol' know nothin' Southern cracker, have when I'm up against the likes of you?"

Tracy was building her comeback. She remembered the stories kids from home would tell of their visits up north and how they had put rude, arrogant Yankees in their place.

"The South will rise again!" they'd declare with a whoop.

She was usually repelled by these displays. She preferred to think of herself as sophisticated, someone who could rise above such pettiness. But now that she was in the thick of one of these face-offs herself she hated to confess she was not only worked up, she was having great fun.

"Do you honestly think," she said as she and Robin scowled at each other, with Angie standing over to one side still grasping the desk chair, "that I am acting any differently than what y'all would have expected from me? You have to admit that as soon as you heard me say hello you automatically thought I'd be a caricature of myself. So I figured, I'll just give these overbearing northerners exactly what they expect. I'll let them sit around like the pompous idiots they are, congratulating themselves on their vast and ill-informed knowledge of the South."

There was no reply from either of them. *Great*, thought Tracy, *I have Robin just where I want her. Maybe I'll ask her if she wants to know how many slaves my daddy owns or if I drink from the Whites Only water fountain in the park.*

But the thought of those questions made Tracy stop. Images of the old South embarrassed her. After all, it wasn't so many years ago. Her parents would have been appalled that she'd even consider saying such things, even in jest. They had always been on the right side of the issue, even back in the sixties when they were teenagers. *And, really*, she wondered, *where does all this get me anyway, especially when I came here thinking I might finally have a chance to be honest?*

A pained look came over her face, and in the quiet her outburst had provoked she once again strode center stage, this time seeking their understanding instead of her own retribution.

Looking down at her feet, she began quietly. "For the past month, I've felt like I was dropped into a foreign country. People speak differently, act differently (mostly rude)," she couldn't resist, "and I am wary of every interaction I have."

Angie looked uneasy and apologetic. Tracy wondered if she was regretting being a part of this entire scene.

"Oh Tracy," she said, "I'm so sorry for ... "

But Tracy was compelled to continue and to get it all out.

"I was hoping you two," she gave Robin a quick turn of her head before looking back at Angie, "could provide me with a rest from all that."

Angie was now staring down at her hands still on the back of the chair, filled with remorse.

Tracy turned fully to Robin. "So I will now answer your question, honestly and directly, as you posed it." She paused for effect. "Girls. Or rather, women. From as far back as I can remember."

Angie looked up, relief and gratitude evident in her slow smile. She took a few steps and hugged Tracy. The image of a lesbian welcome wagon came to her mind and made her smile. Angie wrapped her arms around sagging shoulders and Tracy hugged back, whispering into Angie's neck, "that feels good."

Still seated, Robin appeared to be annoyed and a bit jealous. Tracy looked over and saw a mixture of irritation and confusion on her face. *She's probably wondering if I'm going to replace her as Angie's friend. That's what happens a lot of times when two become three. Someone always gets left out.*

She saw Robin turn away as if she had decided not to care. Angie looked over at the armchair, her dark eyes pleading as she tried to get Robin's attention. Finally she said with some urgency, "Robin, come here."

Tracy turned her attention to the armchair, not knowing what to expect. She nodded to Robin, indicating that she agreed with Angie and whispered, "Please?"

To Tracy's complete surprise, Robin stood up. As she took the three steps necessary to reach them, she leaned forward and their arms encircled her.

"Okay, okay," she sighed and turned to Tracy. "Welcome to the fold." She looked around the room and then back at the two of them. "This is home now; we better make the best of it."

CHAPTER SIX

Patty Coolidge sat at her desk and looked down at her appointment book. *Three p.m., Tracy Patterson.* You didn't have to be Anna Freud to figure out what that one was up to. After teaching for over fifteen years, Patty had learned all the cues and gestures of impending student propositions. While most of them were cute in their crushed-out states, obviously using her as a focus for their own coming out, some were much more forward in their approach. Tracy was definitely one of those. For the last two months, she had been following a deliberate plan of increasing her contact with Patty. Surely today's appointment was thought to be the coup de grace.

The ostensible reason for this visit was Tracy's interest in an independent research assistant assignment, one of the very few Patty gave to freshmen or sophomores. The fact was Tracy Patterson was an excellent student, one of the brightest and most insightful thinkers she'd come across in a long time. When one of the teaching assistants made a point of bringing some short papers Tracy had written to Patty's attention, she was very impressed. Tracy took relatively easy, straightforward assignments and enriched them with information published in research journals, going way beyond what had been asked. If Patty was able to nip this little seduction scene in the bud, she was hoping she could mentor this young student who had the makings of an excellent psychologist.

Well, she thought, as she contemplated today's appointment, at least she'll come away with some of what she wanted.

Patty rested her head in the palm of one hand, her elbow on her mahogany desk. She looked at Jenny's picture positioned at the center directly in front of her. *If I were a man*, she wondered, *and I had a beautiful and*

46

talented young student coming to visit me, would I put that picture away in my desk? As she gazed at Jenny's cap of unruly dark ringlets swept by the wind on the Charles River, Patty melted a little and shook her head sighing.

She swiveled around in her chair to look at another picture that sat on the credenza behind her. It was one of her and Jenny taken over 20 years ago, at the end of high school. She loved the period piece of the photo, both of them in jeans and peasant shirts, looking very 1960s. Patty's hair was down her back and Jenny's dark curls were frizzy and past her shoulders. She noticed how Jenny gazed at her with adoration, the way students like Tracy did now, while Patty looked right at the camera, laughing. *Typical of us then*, she thought. *Such a different picture we'd take now.*

They had known each other all their lives, both coming from well-to-do Boston Brahmin families. After their graduation from the lower school at Buckingham, Browne & Nichols, they'd been sent to the all-girls Winsor School, and then had parted for college—Patty to Vassar and Jenny to Radcliffe. Arriving at the height of the anti-war movement and at the beginning of the women's movement, both of them had become highly politicized and active in a variety of protest activities, some legal and many less so. Their trust fund incomes had financed the difficult lives of many anti-war radicals who'd been forced to live underground.

In those years, while she was not ready to commit to any identity or any one person, Patty had had both male and female lovers. Jenny had been clearer about claiming her love for women. They'd begun sleeping together in high school, but Patty insisted that what they had could never blossom into a real relationship, even though Jenny repeatedly asked for more. This push-pull situation persisted all through college and grad school until Jenny finally had enough and got involved in a series of relationships with other women.

47

It took Patty all those years to finally realize who and what she wanted. This was after she stupidly risked her career in academia by sleeping with one of her students. It had been Jenny who'd forced her to fully comprehend the implications of what she was doing, including the effect it was having on an impressionable, young woman who had come close to committing suicide when Patty broke things off.

Soon after, Patty went west to California on sabbatical and took a hard look at herself. When she returned, she was finally ready to make a commitment to Jenny. But it took Jenny a few more years to believe she was really serious and really ready.

Patty knew now that she'd never take that picture off her desk. She wanted the whole world to know that she and Jenny belonged to one another, especially a student like Tracy who had other ideas. Gazing at the framed photo in front of her, she sighed. *I wasted too many years running away from a relationship with you to jeopardize what we have now, my dear,* she thought. Besides, even if Jenny weren't an issue, she would never again sleep with a student. She'd learned a hard lesson about that a long time ago.

Two firm knocks on the door interrupted her thoughts.

"Come in," she said.

"How are you today, Professor Coolidge?" Tracy asked as she strode confidently toward the desk.

She was dressed impeccably as always in an aqua silk blouse, three buttons open at the top, and soft navy slacks. Not exactly what you'd wear to lounge around the dorm, Patty noted. Tracy's long, blonde hair was smoothed and perfectly brushed, looking so soft Patty had to consciously stop herself from reaching over to touch it.

Realizing that this was going to be tougher than she'd thought and getting hold of herself, Patty responded that she was well and added, "I think you're going to like what I have to tell you today, Tracy, at least some of it."

Tracy smiled and eased into the chair next to Patty's desk, positioning it as close to her as she could get.

"I was wonderin'," she said as she lightly touched the top of Patty's hand, "if I could maybe call you by your first name, of course when we are alone?"

Patty was taken off guard once again. She felt way too drawn into this trap already. Tracy was obviously a pro. Well, she thought, marshaling all her willpower, if ever the direct approach was necessary, this is definitely one of those times.

She leaned back in her desk chair and looked directly into the green eyes that were staring back at her.

"Tracy, I've been here doing what I do for a long time now. I'm over 40 years old and I've been identified as the campus feminist professor, among other things, since the 1980s, when that was not an easy thing to be. What you're doing with me, or trying to do, has been tried before, although certainly not with as much charm as you bring to the task. I had an affair once with a student who was only a little older than you, and it was a mistake that I regret. It's wrong for me in my position here and it's wrong for you."

She paused at that moment, letting what she'd said sink in.

Tracy looked at her intently. Her composure hadn't faded. Patty hoped that her words had registered.

Unexpectedly, Tracy stood, and turned away. "Well I understand you're very busy," she said with a steady voice.

She moved quickly, but before she reached the office door, Patty spoke up.

"Tracy, I wasn't finished. Sit back down. I'd like to talk to you about something that we *can* do together."

#

As Tracy walked back to the dorm, she tried to make sense of what had just happened. Part of her—the part that derived satisfaction from racking up conquests—felt that she still had a shot at Professor Coolidge. *I can break through that outer shell*, she thought. She had noticed that Patty Coolidge had checked her out when she first entered the office, if only for a split second. So she knew there was a physical attraction.

Okay, Tracy reasoned, she once had a bad experience with a student. Well maybe a good one could help her get over it. And it would be very good, no doubt about it.

But another part of Tracy thought about leaving it alone. Professor Coolidge had offered her a research assistant assignment, something that could mark the beginning of what she hoped one day would be a successful career in psychology. This project would give her the chance to really learn something and to be mentored by someone whose intelligence she respected. In offering the position to Tracy, Professor Coolidge had warned her that the work would be "a lot of labor for not a lot of pay." But Tracy knew it was a coveted assignment, something every psych major vied for.

The professor had made Tracy accept the position on the condition that she give up her attempts at seduction. *But maybe I'll just continue to signal my interest and she can go ahead and seduce ME*, she concluded, nodding once more to her conquest side.

She decided that she could let both factions of her win by turning down the volume a bit but not closing off the possibility.

So it was all settled. She could take the research job and save face with her friends. She was actually looking forward to a little Southern-style storytelling when she called Brett tonight.

CHAPTER SEVEN

Somehow the failure of Robin's roommate to appear had not come to the attention of the college authorities, which gave her what she referred to as a "single by default." Rather than use the situation as an opportunity to hide from the world like a latter day J. D. Salinger, she offered up the room as home base—a place where she, Angie and even Tracy could take refuge. This enabled Angie to score big points with her roommate who got the room to herself whenever her hockey player boyfriend visited from Georgetown. This arrangement helped to quiet the gossip mill about Angie, because her roommate now told everyone that Angie was "so helpful and reasonable."

All three of them agreed that they liked Tracy's roommate Barbara, an earnest and serious anthropology major from San Francisco, who had traveled extensively with her college professor parents collecting small wooden sculptures and multi-colored wall hangings that now adorned their room. Over dinner one night, Tracy had told them that Barbara was one of the few people at school who could talk intelligently about the South, having spent a semester in New Orleans with her parents while they were visiting professors at Tulane. She had accompanied them on research excursions all over the region and grew to love the lush vegetation of the Mississippi Delta, the sweet peaches freshly baked into pies, and the stories she had happily gathered of everyday people that usually began "My granddaddy once told me...."

Barbara was often invited to hang out at Robin's and to eat meals with them. They all figured that because she was from San Francisco, she was used to living among gay people. She told them that she would revel in her status as the token straight girl in the group, and in turn, Tracy and Angie set out on a quest to find the quiet, studious Barbara a boyfriend.

#

One morning in November, Robin sat on her bed writing, preferring to spend her time finishing a short story to sitting through another insipid sociology class. Tracy was off doing research for Professor Coolidge and the night before, Angie had gone over to Harvard to watch a women's basketball game with her best friend from high school who was a student there. Robin was relieved to have this time to herself without the worry of being interrupted.

She'd made a point to remind Tracy and Angie that anyone who forced her to stop writing would pay a high price by having to endure an unending amount of grumpiness and resentment. A few weeks before, disregarding her signal of a raised hand, something she had reminded her friends about over and over, Angie and Tracy had pulled Robin off the bed, each dragging her up by the arms. What they had thought would be a pleasant afternoon knocking around the little shops near campus on a rare sunny day, turned out to be pure misery. Robin had been unforgiving and had endlessly harangued them for taking her away from her writing.

"Why would you do that when I raised my hand and told you to wait?" she asked repeatedly. "Now it's all gone and it's going to take me hours to get it back."

She refused to explain the "it" that she had lost, mostly because she could hardly explain it to herself. "It" was a state of mind, a kind of writing trance that made her feel like the mere medium through which stories were told and characters were born and died. She had a method for getting herself to that place and for coming down from it. But when she was cut off, she always had trouble returning to that exact state of mind and to the trajectory of her story.

53

Sitting cross-legged on her bed, her body bent over a notebook, Robin heard a loud *twack* as the door to her room hit the wall with great force. She jerked her free arm up, her fingers straight and rigid in the gesture that said, "Halt!" With her head down, she kept writing.

This time, as she kept her hand in the air, Angie waited, though Robin could tell that her friend could hardly stand still. Angie folded and unfolded her hands repeatedly and breathed out audibly, obviously impatient.

At last Robin lowered her hand, looked up and calmly asked, "So how was the game? Did you survive a night at perfect Harvard?"

As Robin stared at Angie's huge grin, she remembered that a while back Angie had confessed that her original life plan had called for her to go to Harvard as a way of amassing the kind of contacts she'd need later in her political career. But when she received her rejection from the one place she'd spent years dreaming about on the exact same day she was notified that she'd won a coveted full scholarship to Adams, an honor bestowed on only one Boston-area student, she made her decision.

"My life plan will just have to be amended to include Adams," she had said with conviction as Robin sat there shaking her head and smiling.

Robin had been incredulous that someone would be so calculating as to actually have a life plan. But Angie insisted that it was no different from Robin's own aspirations to learn the techniques and discipline she'd need to write great fiction.

"You came to Adams so you could work with three writers you admired," she said.

"Yes, but to learn from them, not to make business contacts."

"And if Joe Donovan introduced you to a publisher, would you refuse to meet with them?"

"No, of course not," Robin said. "But … that's different."

Angie shrugged. "I don't see how."

Now Angie was bouncing up and down on the balls of her feet. Relieved to move her body at last, she bounded for the bed, sending shock waves toward Robin as she jumped onto the mattress and drew her knees to her chest, moving her rear end up and down for effect.

"Robin Greene," she said, shaking the bed with her rapid movements, "you should consider yourself the luckiest person on earth, (well actually maybe the second luckiest, after me) because you get to hear this first!"

She was speaking rapidly, still moving, the vibrations causing Robin to grab onto the blanket and sheets to steady herself.

She looked at Angie wide-eyed.

"What is this? Stop. I'm getting seasick," she said in mock annoyance. And then with a smile added, "You know how I feel about enthusiasm."

Angie grinned back, "So then I guess you have no interest in hearing about the best sex I have ever had in my entire life?"

A short guffaw escaped Robin's mouth.

"You met a basketball player," she said, her head tilted. It was a statement and not a question.

"I met THE basketball player," came the excited reply.

Robin rolled her eyes, but in the next few minutes sat riveted as Angie explained how she had fallen for Harvard's center, Nicky Ford, at first glimpse and had waited for her at the locker room door, immediately engaging her in conversation. She'd ignored her friend's warnings that Nicky had been breaking hearts up and down the freshman class and was major trouble.

Angie had just replied, "I want trouble and I want it now!"

55

Laughing out loud, Robin covered her face with her hand and shook her head. She was fascinated and a little surprised at Angie's aggressiveness though she was starting to understand where that drive to be a great politician came from. Despite being the sweet and pleasant type, Angie had a well of ambition; a forceful, insistent ambition that focused her and propelled her toward her goal. It appeared to also kick into high gear when it came to this crazy jock thing she had.

But in that moment there was little space for more reflection. Angie was talking nonstop, describing how Nicky was from New York City and had gone to a chic-sounding private school in Manhattan. She explained that Nicky hated her parents, had rebelled all her life, laying waste to every social nicety and convention her mother imposed on her. Messy, impulsive, disorganized, and brilliant, she was a misfit among blue blazer-clad perfect children.

Robin rolled her eyes thinking, *poor little rich girl*.

Angie ignored Robin and continued her monologue. When Nicky had finally found basketball, everything began to come together for her and she excelled. She played with prep school kids as well as with a group of girls from the inner city neighborhoods of New York.

As Angie went on, Robin did nothing to hide her negative reactions. She was also trying to remember if she'd ever met Nicky or someone like her in the city. But Robin had hooked up with street queers, not jocks. Their paths had never crossed.

Angie then went on and on about politics, describing Nicky's interest in campaigns and her work for a liberal Congresswoman from the Bronx who was one of Angie's heroes. She explained that Nicky lived for campaigning the way she lived for basketball. Angie had been thrilled when Nicky asked her about local politics in Massachusetts and she'd been able to tell her about the state's current budget problems and the last elections.

56

Nicky then dazzled Angie with her theories about demographic trends and generational party loyalties.

Softly at first and then louder, Robin started singing an old song called Daddy's Money.

You can always count on your daddy's money

You can always count on your daddy's money

"Just what the world needs, another wealthy politician," she said.

"No," Angie responded, so earnest that Robin let out the longest sigh she could muster. "She's going to be a campaign consultant, someone who works for politicians."

Robin shook her head and raised her hand once again in the "Halt" gesture. "Well, I'm sure I could listen to you go on and on about politics for another three hours," she said, "but really, all I actually want to know is how was the sex?"

"Terrific, the best," Angie said, grinning.

"You mean based on your scientific sample of just one other person?"

"Two. I slept with somebody last summer when my friend Marla and I went to Ptown."

"Oh my, my, my, Angie Antonelli, I never had you pegged as a one night stand kinda girl," Robin said with a note of approval in her voice.

"Well, it was Ptown, my last summer before college, Marla got picked up first, and I figured, why not?" Angie said. She squared her shoulders and looked directly at Robin. The expression 'proud as a peacock' came to mind.

Robin closed her right hand and held it up to Angie's mouth, pretending it was a microphone.

"And how were your polling numbers after the one night stand, Senator?" she asked with a smirk.

But Angie could not be provoked by Robin's usual smart-ass remarks, not today.

"They actually went up," she said. Robin chuckled, thinking again of the peacock. Continuing her interview, Robin moved the imaginary microphone to her own mouth.

"Well, so then, we have a scientific sample of three. And based on that extraordinarily large number of women with whom you've done the deed, Nicky, if you'll excuse the expression, comes out on top."

Drawing her knees up to her chest and wrapping her arms around them, Robin asked, "Why was it so terrific?"

Angie sighed. "You are not getting a play-by-play. Suffice it to say, bells rang, firecrackers went off, all of that stuff."

"Great orgasms, huh?"

"I'm not doing this with you!" Angie said in a singsong voice, this time raising her own hand to say halt. "Just because you and Tracy do not hesitate to go into the greatest level of detail describing all sorts of things to me, doesn't mean I'm going to do the same thing."

"Okay, okay," Robin said. "Just tell me this. How many times? I mean, how many last night and how many this morning? Was it plain old vanilla sex or something more interesting?" Robin raised her eyebrows in an exaggerated gesture.

"You're too much. Do you really think I would tell you these things?"

Robin looked at her seriously trying to stifle a laugh.

"Angie, you don't understand," she said, "I am giving you an opportunity …"

The laughter broke through and Robin couldn't continue.

Angie looked at her with her skeptical smile and then began to laugh as well.

Catching her breath, Robin continued, "… an opportunity to talk openly about sex and to ask questions of someone who is infinitely more experienced than you."

Angie was laughing and trying to talk.

"I am so sorry I misunderstood," she said, getting the words out with some effort. "I didn't realize you were here to help me, oh great experienced one. I just thought you were in it for the juicy details."

The door opened and Tracy walked in.

"I could hear y'all laughing from out in the hall. What's going on?"

Robin pointed at Angie. "Our friend here …"

Angie extended her leg and kicked Robin's shin repeatedly.

"Oww!" Robin pulled her leg closer in, moving out of range. "Our friend here got lucky last night."

Tracy looked confused for a second and then smiled. Joining them on the bed, she looked Angie in the eye and said, "Well, then tell me all about it and don't leave anything out."

Robin laughed and looked directly at Tracy in her dark pink, long sleeved scoop-necked shirt and tight designer jeans. That initial attraction she'd felt at the hall meeting back in September had not gone away. If anything, it had intensified. Once she took notice of Tracy, it was always hard to look away, but she forced herself because, she reasoned, no good could come of this. Tracy never looked back at her the same way.

"Well," Robin said, glancing back at Tracy, "maybe you'll have more luck than I did getting her to give up the goods."

Tracy's face was serious as she turned to Angie.

"It's sometimes helpful to talk about these things with someone who's had more experience," she said, her voice dripping with sympathy as she put her hand on Angie's shoulder.

Robin smiled and shook her head.

"I already tried that tactic."

Angie stood up from the bed and looked at both of them.

"As you can imagine I'm sure, I had very little sleep last night and it's beginning to catch up with me. I'm gonna go lay down before my afternoon class."

She spoke to Tracy as she walked out of the room. "Robin can fill you in."

It was one of the rare times that they found themselves alone together without Angie. Robin looked at Tracy and then down at the bed, playing with the edge of the sheet. Tracy looked at her expectantly.

"So who is it and what sport does she play?"

"Rich, New York City private school kid, goes to Harvard. Basketball."

Tracy crinkled her nose and made the kind of face you'd make if you ate something that tasted awful.

"What could she be thinking?"

"I don't know," Robin replied, "but I can guarantee you that she was thinking with a body part that was certainly not her brain."

She looked at Tracy who was smiling at her and nodding. For a long minute, neither of them looked away.

CHAPTER EIGHT

The last few weeks of finals and papers had been intense. Tracy, Robin, and Angie spent hours together in Robin's room studying and writing. A few times, while Angie had run off to Harvard to see Nicky, Tracy and Robin worked side by side, talking mostly about their schoolwork but occasionally sliding in little stories about their lives back home. Robin was writing a paper for her European history course on the rise of the German nation state and early antecedents of German nationalism and anti-Semitism. Tracy was muddling through a paper on Jane Austen, pleading with Robin for help in spotting themes and deeper meanings.

Robin had been surprisingly patient with her and spent hours calmly talking her through the trials of Emma and Mr. Knightley, as well as Elizabeth and Darcy. She'd written a paper on Austen in high school for AP English and knew the author inside out. In an effort to reassure Tracy that her help would be of some value, Robin explained that her teacher had submitted the paper to a contest held by the US chapter of some Jane Austen club and it had won an award.

They'd stayed up until two in the morning one night discussing *Pride and Prejudice* and *Emma*, which Robin had heard was being made into a film called *Clueless*, which would be set in an American high school.

"Not sure how that's gonna work," she told Tracy.

"Listen, I really appreciate what you're doing," Tracy said as she turned off the light and lay down on the spare bed in Robin's room. "This paper would have been pure trash without you."

"Well, just be glad you weren't writing about Dostoyevsky," said Robin as she turned out the light. "I haven't gotten up to speed on the Russians yet. But that's coming."

Tracy wriggled out of her black leggings and pulled the covers over the Adams t-shirt she was wearing, wondering why she hadn't walked ten feet down the hall to her own room. She lay awake watching Robin write in her journal using a pen that had a small light on it, something she had found at the Coop in Harvard Square.

"I'm sorry, is this keeping you up?" Robin asked, referring to the pinprick of light emitted by the pen.

Tracy realized she'd been caught watching.

"No, it's fine, I'll just turn over. Good night."

Tracy lay awake awhile longer, listening to the scratch of Robin's writing, the soft fall of the notebook as it hit the floor, and then Robin's breathing. For a few seconds she wondered what it would feel like to sleep with Robin's back tucked into her chest, their arms entwined. She smiled to herself, imagining the sun on their faces as they woke up together in the morning, their bodies close and warm, touching. Surprised and alarmed, she shook her head to dislodge these crazy thoughts, closed her eyes, and finally dropped off to sleep.

#

December in North Carolina seemed almost tropical after the harsh twenty-degree days of Boston. It hadn't snowed yet at home so the brown, chunky Kenneth Cole boots Tracy was wearing didn't really seem necessary. She slipped them off onto the white tiled floor of the entryway just inside her house, leaving her suitcase there as well.

As she walked into the large living room on her way to find her mother, she felt almost empty and at a loss for direction. Four weeks at home with almost nothing to do felt strange. It would begin with

Christmas and all the craziness that entailed. She hadn't bought one present for anyone yet and the malls would be a madhouse. She also had to finish a short paper for the research project she was doing for Professor Coolidge. She could use her Adams ID to get into the Duke library for that. But it was only a few afternoons of work. What was she going to do for almost three weeks in January?

There were high school friends she didn't really want to see other than Brett and Jeff. Everyone would be home from school just like her and she couldn't bear to return to a life filled with lies. She and Brett had agreed they would tell people at home they were no longer dating but remained close friends.

There was also Millicent to avoid. Tracy had no interest in starting that up again, though she wasn't exactly clear why. It might be good to catch up on all the sex she wasn't having at school, but the thought of being with Millicent no longer appealed to her.

What's going on with me? she wondered.

"Hiiiii Tracy, welcome home." Her mother swept into the room and gave her a quick hug and kiss on the cheek. Her honey blonde hair was up in a clip off her neck and her usual perfume permeated the room. She put her hands on Tracy's shoulders and stepped back.

"Let me take a good look at you."

She stared at Tracy's face and frowned. "Maybe a little makeup? You're looking mighty pale."

"Momma, what do you expect?" Tracy said with a hint of exasperation in her voice. "There's hardly any sun in Boston and when there is, it's too cold to go out."

Loosening her grip on Tracy's shoulders, her mother reached for the two hands at her daughter's side. Bringing them together, she looked at Tracy's bitten down nails and cuticles and shook her head in dismay.

63

"Tracy, your nails are still frightful. Let's get you in to see Priscilla at the salon for a manicure before Christmas."

Tracy closed her eyes and tilted her head up, exhaling audibly.

"Congratulations Momma. You got to my nails within two minutes of my arrival. A new world record for you."

"And you should be grateful that I did. After all, what boy is going to want to hold a hand that looks like this?"

None, I hope, thought Tracy. *And no girl or woman, for that matter, has given me one word of grief over it.*

With Tracy's high grades, good looks, fake boyfriend and unacceptable level of popularity, there was very little that Luanne Patterson could disapprove of in her daughter except her bitten down nails. Tracy reasoned that her mother had latched onto this one little flaw for dear life in order to have something she could find worth disapproving, never realizing that her otherwise perfect daughter was getting into gay bars at seventeen with a fake ID and sleeping with a succession of older women. Luanne never questioned Tracy when she came home very late from a night out that had begun with Brett picking her up at home and charming Luanne while he waited for Tracy to come downstairs. There was even a little hug and kiss hello that was staged in front of her parents, just to make the deception even more believable.

As Christmas neared, Tracy told Brett and Jeff about her unease being back home and enlisted their help to try to figure out why she felt so unsettled. She joked that she had named this trip The Avoidance Holiday, with much of her energy devoted to keeping away from a multitude of people she didn't want to see. Brett had simply chalked this up to typical re entry from college and figured he wasn't feeling the same way because he hadn't gone to school so far from home. Jeff, who normally said very little,

64

stared at Tracy for a long time from his seat on the couch across the room and simply said, "You're changing."

Brett looked at him quizzically and sat down next to Jeff.

"Baby, why do you say that? She seems the same to me."

Jeff merely shrugged his big shoulders, put his arm around Brett, and faced him.

"She's not," he said. "She's impatient."

"Jeffy's right," Tracy spoke up from across the room. "I just wish I knew for what."

In the spirit of The Avoidance Holiday, Tracy stayed away from the insane malls and did her Christmas shopping in the small Chapel Hill stores near UNC. She picked up gifts for family fairly quickly, not giving her selections a great deal of thought. But she spent hours wandering the funky stores looking for just the right gifts for her friends.

Brett and Jeff got lightweight cashmere sweaters. Brett's a slate blue to match his eyes and Jeff's a forest green to complement his dark brown coloring. At the campus bookstore, which was a Borders, she found the complete collection of Armistead Maupin's *Tales of the City* books, which she bought as a joint gift for them. Her roommate, Barbara, was getting the book by the Delany sisters, two 100-year-old African American siblings who'd grown up in the post-Reconstruction South. And Angie would get three books—a new collection of poems by Audre Lorde; Laura Esquivel's *Like Water for Chocolate*, which she thought Angie would like for its focus on ethnic food; and a new biography of Franklin Roosevelt that covered his years in office prior to World War II.

All she had left was Robin. Books made sense, but Robin was a voracious reader and Tracy worried that she was already home on Long Island reading anything Tracy might find for her at Borders. She thought about a nice journal or an expensive pen, but Robin was way too picky about the instruments of her writing and Tracy worried she would choose something that would never get used. The last thing she wanted was to have Robin look quickly at her gift, mumble, "Thanks, it's nice" and then look away. She didn't think she could handle that.

She walked the streets of Chapel Hill unhappy with everything she saw. Even now, hundreds of miles away, Robin was problematic.

She drove around the college town aimlessly, trying to put her mind to the task. Clothing was out of the question. Robin's only coveted garment was her leather jacket. She never wore anything other than faded blue or black jeans, t-shirts and threadbare button down shirts. Tracy thought about CDs. Robin already owned everything the Indigo Girls had recorded and their new CD wasn't due out until spring. There were punk and grunge bands she liked, but Tracy had no interest in immersing herself in music she detested. There was also Robin's attachment to Robert Mapplethorpe. Tracy wondered if she could find a print and have it framed. But how likely would it be that she'd find something by a sexually explicit gay photographer, even in Chapel Hill?

As she tossed around all these ideas, discarding most of them, she noticed a handwritten sign on the side of the road. *Swap Meet Today, 9–6.* She'd been to this weekend outdoor sell-a-thon before. It was usually held in the warmer months, but made a brief appearance before Christmas. Most of the stuff sold was junk: costume jewelry, old kitchen appliances and dinnerware, tables filled with cheap socks and men's boxers. She pulled the car into the gravel lot that lined the shoulder of the road and decided to try her luck.

Much of it was just what she expected, but she made her way up and down the makeshift aisles and scanned the tables crowded with other people's crap. Once in a while she saw a slipshod display of posters or books and stopped to look more closely. As she strolled down the last aisle, preparing to get back on the road and resume her search, she saw another table sporting piles of books and a stack of flattened posters. She stopped and began to sort through the offerings, uncomfortable that a large man in a leather jacket, his head wrapped in a red bandanna, was leering at her.

"See anything you like, sweetheart?" he asked.

She looked up to see him towering over her, his blonde beard and moustache twitching as he smirked. Tracy looked down at the books she was combing through.

"Nothing so far," she said in a weary voice, hoping he'd get the double meaning.

A second figure walked up to him and leaned against his arm and shoulder. Tracy looked up and saw a tall, thin woman also in a leather jacket and bandanna. Her long, wavy, rust-colored hair was tied back. She looked at Tracy and then up at the guy and scowled.

"Give the little girl some space, sugar," she said, pulling him with her to the other end of the table.

Tracy knew that the woman had acted out of needless jealousy, but she was relieved to no longer have the guy breathing down her neck. She was about to abandon the books she'd gone through, as well as this table and the entire swap meet, when she noticed two boxes of books at her feet. She squatted down and pulled up the flaps of cardboard on top to look at the contents inside. There was a packing label on one of the flaps with the words "Estate of Nanette Carlisle" written on it in blue marker.

She began to look closely but couldn't avoid thinking that she was on the most pointless mission of this lengthy day and once again wished Robin was less difficult. There were long-forgotten novels, travel memoirs, and large coffee table books with photographs of the Sistine Chapel and the Dutch Masters. *This is truly futile*, she thought.

She opened the other box, finding a book on astronomy, probably written before the invention of the telescope, and next to it three thin volumes wrapped together in a clear plastic sleeve. She pulled the books out of the box and looked at the title of the first one. *Emma* by Jane Austen. She slid off the plastic and opened the book. The title page said, "Emma, A Novel in Three Volumes," and at the bottom of the page, "London, Printed for John Murray, 1816." Attached to the page by a tiny paper clip was a slip of paper and on it was written in a shaky script, "First edition." Tracy's eyes were wide and her mouth agape. Could it really be?

She put the books back into the plastic sleeve and stood up with the three wrapped books in her hands, feeling light headed and slightly afraid. Why were these hidden away in a box under the table along with a bunch of old, worthless books? She looked back through both boxes but found nothing else that came close to the treasure she had accidently stumbled upon. And then she remembered the packing label on the box. This book had belonged to the now dead Nanette Carlisle. It was likely packed up carelessly with everything else she owned and sold to this couple at an estate sale. Those guys had no idea what this was and how much it was worth, and Tracy was not about to tell them. Not when she'd finally found the perfect gift for Robin.

She quickly grabbed two other books, the large art book of Dutch Masters and a worn hardcover copy of Carson McCullers' *A Member of the Wedding*, a book she'd read in high school.

She walked over to the other side of the table to pay the woman, trying to avoid the guy. He came right over to her and bent forward with only the table between them.

"Watcha got beautiful?"

"Three books," she said.

The woman leaned over and stared at the books. She looked up at Tracy and was angry.

"I bet you use that pretty face of yours to pull the wool over people's eyes all the time, dontcha?"

Tracy looked confused and worried. While it was clear that the guy had no idea about the book, maybe the woman knew?

"Charge her for five books, Troy." She pointed to the three-book set. "I don't care if those three are all wrapped together. She's gotta pay for each one."

The guy had a sheepish look on his face.

"That'll be ten dollars, sweetheart."

Relief flooded through Tracy's body and she dug into her bag for her wallet, handing him a ten-dollar bill.

She carried the books back to her car, and as she passed the last table crowded with children's used toys and old clocks, she placed the large art book on the edge. She decided though that she couldn't bear to have Carson McCullers meet the same fate and she kept *Member of the Wedding* in her hands along with the three remarkable first edition volumes of *Emma*.

She had a momentary pang of guilt, wondering if she should attempt to find the family of Nanette Carlisle to let them know about the valuable item that had so cavalierly been sold out from under them. But, as she put the car in gear and backed out onto the road, she quickly decided to let things be. Driving toward home she smiled, thinking of the look on Robin's face when she opened the gift.

#

The letdown after Christmas, with all its activity and hoopla, was particularly difficult for Tracy knowing she still had three weeks left at home. She worked on her psych research project and hid out at the movies, seeing *Mrs. Doubtfire* with Brett and Jeff and a foreign film, *The*

Piano, with her parents. She spent an afternoon and evening alone at the art house in Chapel Hill sitting through *What's Eating Gilbert Grape* twice. She loved the quirky imperfection of the characters, particularly the endearing, slow-witted younger brother who kept climbing the town's water tower every time somebody wasn't watching him. Tracy felt comforted by this eccentric family and she imagined herself at school watching the film with Angie and Robin. Angie would adore the sentimentality of small town life and the offbeat love story about Gilbert and the girl who moves to his town. Robin would cheer for the flawed characters—the 500-pound mother who never left the house, and like Tracy, the rebellious little brother. She could almost imagine Robin joining in the boy's obsession, racing him to the top of the water tower, and both of them refusing to come down.

As she watched the closing credits at the end of the second showing, her mouth a little stiff from eating too much popcorn and washing it down with Diet Coke, she realized that her two new friends had taken up residence inside her— Angie, with her friendly openness and romantic dreams, and Robin, with her defiant and brash directness and her deep intellect. These were girls she wouldn't have given a second look in high school, and yet, here they were center stage in her life, even when they were far away in their northern cities.

She again wondered what to make of all this change and of Jeff's astute observation that she was impatient for something. The movies and the research paper had staved off that impatience temporarily, but it stubbornly returned and her body felt tense and wired for who knew what.

I need sex, she concluded. Luckily New Year's Eve was only a few days away.

Brett had talked her into going to a New Year's party in Raleigh hosted by people he'd met through the gay and lesbian student group at

70

Duke. He assured her there'd be girls as well as boys, and that if it was really dull, they could duck out to the mixed gay bar in town. She, Brett, and Jeff had rejected invitations to parties given by their high school friends.

Tracy had originally thought she'd stick close to home, go to the women's bar and pick someone up for the night. She was a little concerned that this party in Raleigh was not going to get her what she wanted, so she told Brett she'd follow along in her own car in case she wanted to return to Durham and go back to her original plan.

"You know I don't do well with my own age group," she told him.

"Well honey, maybe the host's mother will come home early and you'll get lucky. Or maybe you'll meet up with the mother's best friend," he said.

"Not funny," she replied, though she was silently laughing to herself. *I deserved that one*, she thought. "Okay, I'll go, but if I don't get some relief soon, I'm going to explode."

"Well let's hope that happens in a good way, sweetie."

"Let's hope," she said.

The house, in a suburban subdivision, was a classic 1950s split-level. Enter through the front door and up a short flight of stairs to the living room, and then back down and down more stairs to the basement. When they got there around ten, the place was packed, which cheered Tracy. Jeff trailed in a little behind them, having confided his worries that he'd be the only black person there. Tracy noticed an Indian girl headed down the stairs as he was going up. They looked at each other and smiled. *Cute, but too young for me*, she thought.

"We the only people with the natural tans here?" Jeff asked the girl.

"Practically," she said, "but I did see a couple of your sisters and brothers around, though none of mine."

"Hmm," he said, "I'll keep a look out for you and let you know if I spot any."

Tracy walked into the kitchen, poured herself a vodka tonic and drank it quickly. She then refilled her glass with just soda water and walked around. She'd outfitted herself for the night in a tight-fitting, very short, black dress that hugged her hips and showed off legs toned by fifteen years of dance classes. The bodice of the dress was black lace and the straps thin satin, suggesting a slip. It ended at the top of her breasts, displaying a hint of cleavage. Her hair was down, falling right past her shoulders.

Not wanting to be mistaken for straight, which was a problem for the feminine lesbians she'd run into in the bars, she noticeably checked out every woman in the crowd. Many looked back, but as she'd suspected, they were around her age and not all that interesting. She decided to try her luck downstairs, and if nothing materialized, to bug Brett about making their exit to the bar.

The basement of the house was very dark, lit only by a few strings of tiny white Christmas lights. The music, which had floated upstairs at a decent level, was deafening down there and people were dancing. Once her eyes adjusted, she searched out the women, put down her glass and moved to the center of the floor to dance near a group that had bunched together without noticeable pairings. It felt good to move her body and to see the looks of appreciation on the faces around her. She danced like that for about fifteen minutes until the music slowed down and she decided it was time for another drink. As she approached a counter lined with clear, amber, and green bottles, she tried to find the vodka, looking closely in the dark for the right label.

"What can I get you?" a voice asked in her ear.

She turned to face the source and saw a taller woman with short dark hair buzzed on the sides and spiky on top. She appeared to be a little older than the girls Tracy had seen upstairs, so she decided to investigate.

"Hmm, what can you get me?" she asked back with a smile. "There's a dangerous question."

The woman smiled. "Let's start with a drink. How 'bout that?"

"Okay, then, vodka and tonic."

"You're more of a vodka girl than a gin girl, I take it?"

"Vodka has fewer calories."

"Which is how you're able to fit into that dress, I suppose? Not that I'm complaining."

Tracy looked right into the woman's eyes. "I'm Tracy."

"Dana. Pleased to meet you Tracy," she said as she began to reach for the tall, rectangular bottle of vodka.

Dana was dressed casually in black jeans and sneakers, a white button down shirt and a black suit vest, a look Tracy loved on a woman. After she handed Tracy her drink, they talked for a little while on the sidelines, sitting close and speaking into one another's ears to be heard over the music. The conversation topics were the typical pre-pickup subjects. Do you live around here? Where do you go to school? Did you come alone or with anyone? Tracy managed through them effortlessly, deciding after a few minutes that this Dana, a North Carolina State grad student who had an apartment off campus, would be a perfectly adequate way to ring in 1994, provided she could pass the dance test.

Tracy could always get a clue about how a woman would be in bed by the way she danced. She knew this wasn't exactly foolproof. She was sure there were plenty of bad dancers who were great sex partners, and vice versa, but she'd always enjoyed this little game of hers, trying to predict prowess between the sheets by assessing someone's performance on the dance floor.

Back at school, as the semester was ending, she had convinced Angie and Robin to go dancing to let off steam after all their hard work. Angie had brought Nicky along and the two of them danced for a while and then walked over to a dark corner together. Tracy stood to the side watching Robin dance with someone. Robin's fluid movements and intuitive feeling for the music were a shocking surprise. Her body seemed to almost change shape when she danced. She seemed taller and more, more, what? Sexy? In control! Hot! *Wow*, thought Tracy transfixed as she stared at Robin's hips rocking in a smooth and natural back and forth rhythm, *she must be amazing in bed*. Even just considering that silently was enough to make Tracy blush and turn away. She was uncomfortably warm and she couldn't help but notice an ache between her legs. She headed to the front of the bar for a quick reprieve outside the door to get some cold night air. *Where did that come from*, she wondered?

As she and Dana now danced facing one another, the word "adequate" again came to Tracy's mind. Dana wasn't a great dancer but she moved her body nicely and kept the rhythm of the music. By the time the DJ slowed things down and they drew close to one another to dance, Tracy was ready to nudge the evening forward. She leaned her head on Dana's left shoulder and lightly kissed her neck causing Dana to shiver and hold on tighter. That gave Tracy the signal she needed.

"Is your apartment nearby?" she asked in Dana's ear.

Dana pulled her head up and just nodded, prompting a sly smile from Tracy, who tilted her head to the side and said, "good, let's go."

Dana took her hand and led her upstairs where she ran into Brett and Jeff on their way down. Brett looked at Dana, saw her grasp on Tracy's hand and turned to his friend with a question on his face. Tracy gave him a slight nod, their usual signal. Brett caught it and smiled, mouthing, "have fun" as Tracy was pulled past him.

As they stepped into Dana's apartment, Tracy was surprised to discover that the suave, smooth woman at the party was a bit more shy than Tracy would have predicted. So she found herself taking charge, making the first move to kiss, get undressed and run her hands over Dana's body. Once they were in bed, she finally took Dana's hand, moved it between her legs and whispered, "I want you. Why don't you see how much?"

She felt her arousal building, but forced herself not to grab Dana's tentative hand to get exactly what she wanted. Instead, she relaxed her body and closed her eyes. Immediately the vision of Robin dancing came back to her and she pictured it clearly in her mind, except this time she was the one on the dance floor with Robin. Their eyes locked, their bodies moving in the exact same way. Forgetting where she was and what was happening, Tracy focused intently on the imagined dance and the pressure building between her legs. The scene was vivid in front of her, Robin's fluid movements and her knowing smile. As Robin thrust her hips forward, Tracy leaned back slightly and then moved her hips in Robin's direction in time to the music while Robin leaned back. They repeated this rocking motion several times lost in one another's eyes. The vision lifted Tracy higher and higher to where she needed to get. The same thought then entered her mind as it had when she stood watching Robin from the sidelines—*she must be amazing in bed.* It propelled her forward over the crest of her climb and into her release, what she'd needed for days, for weeks. It was powerful and it had nothing to do with the woman in the bed who was now holding her and whispering, "You're incredible."

Tracy kept her eyes closed until she knew it would be impolite to do so any longer. She smiled at Dana and said, "It's only right that I thank you properly."

She knew what she had to do and she made quick work of it. Dana surged under her tongue and Tracy got some satisfaction from the woman's pleasure. But after the obligatory cuddling, she swung her legs out of bed and reached for her dress sitting like a puddle on the floor, explaining that her parents would expect her home and she couldn't stay the night.

The half-hour drive back to Durham was disorienting. How could she have come so hard fantasizing about Robin? What could that mean? She'd never even thought about Robin that way.

It must be the dancing. She'd just gotten caught up in that memory.

As she turned onto her darkened street, she thought about how difficult this winter break had been. She missed Robin and Angie so much. They had grounded her life, given her a safe harbor where she could be herself. They valued her brain and her sense of humor more than her looks. She decided that all of this weird stuff, including tonight, must be connected to the re-entry thing that Brett had been talking about. She was sure of it. It couldn't be about anything else. Robin was just her friend, nothing more.

Well, she reasoned, *at least the sex, however strange, made me feel a little more relaxed. And there's only two weeks to go until I see her, I mean, them.*

The time inched by and Tracy did her best to keep busy. She read a lot, saw more movies and called Angie a few times. They both agreed that they couldn't wait to get back to Adams.

"Pretty strange," Tracy said, "since none of us wanted to go there in the first place." She was including Robin in this observation.

Angie laughed. "I know. But back then, I didn't realize that you guys would be there. Now it feels more like home than, well, home."

As she approached the final weekend of the break, Tracy was finally able to lose the sense of dread she'd lived with since returning to Durham and replace it with anticipation. She'd be flying up to Boston on Sunday, so

76

on Saturday she began the process of getting her things together and preparing for the trip. As she repacked her suitcase, she was interrupted when her mother poked her head in the room.

"Tracy, please don't make any plans this evening. Millicent and Bradley, Junior are joining us for dinner."

Tracy closed her eyes and breathed out audibly.

"Momma, I was hoping to see Brett tonight."

"There'll be plenty of time for that later in the evening. And besides, you told me you and he aren't dating any longer and I thought you might enjoy some time with Bradley."

"Momma, Brett is still my closest friend here and I'm leaving tomorrow to go back to school." She said this as she stood with her hands firmly on her hips and then let out a sigh. "Okay, I'll do dinner and see Brett after. But, you know, Bradley has a girlfriend up in Philadelphia."

"Oh, Tracy, that's not serious. It's not gonna last."

Tracy closed her eyes and shook her head in response. "I'll do the dinner but that's all. Maybe Bradley will come out with Brett and me afterward, but only as a friend."

"That sounds very nice, dear. Millicent will be so pleased."

Oh Momma, she thought, *you have no idea what really pleases Millicent.*

CHAPTER NINE

Robin had to admit that it was a relief to be back at school and still have her room to herself. She'd been worried throughout the break that Adams would foist a transfer student or a late-starting freshman onto her. But so far, after a few days back, no stranger had barged in with suitcases and boxes. With classes starting the next day, she worried that it could still happen, but she was feeling a little more secure at this point.

She'd done a bit of writing at home, sitting in her mother's pottery studio, one of her favorite places to write, amid mounds of soft clay and shards of discarded ceramic. Years ago, her father had converted the two-car garage into a studio. With her mother's blessing, Robin and her younger brother Adam had adopted it as their own playroom. Her mother had loved working at her pottery wheel with the kids under foot when they were little, all their toys mixed in with the tubes of glaze and the shaping tools. Her only rule was that they had to stay away from the hot kiln at the back and she and Robin's father had put up all kinds of dividers and gates to create a barrier. Robin never went near there, preferring to keep her hands in the unformed clay and to spin the wheel around when she wasn't reading or writing little stories.

Adam, four years younger, shaped small animals out of clay and later graduated to the wheel, clearly inheriting their mother's considerable artistic talent. Even now, at fifteen, Adam had begun to show signs of becoming an accomplished potter. Wendy was able to sell some of his work on consignment. He always received his ten percent to spend as he wished while the rest went into a college fund.

The studio continued to be a refuge and Robin had set up a desk and chair for her writing. It felt peaceful and safe to work alongside her mother. She'd finished two short stories over the break and was eager to show them to Joe, who'd be working with her this coming semester.

In addition to the stories, Robin also kept up her journals. As far back as she could remember she'd always been on the sidelines, observing and recording. Like an artist with a giant sketchpad and charcoals, Robin contemplated form. She studied understated, subtle gestures like the gentle nod of a head, the raising of a finger to the chin, or a swallow shimmying down the throat. She was driven to perfect a narrative of the body, to convey its lines and curves, its bulges and bumps.

It had been fun to decode Angie's lexicon of smiles; to see how her dark, layered hair swayed and rustled in the wake of a grin or a pursed-lip flirtation; to observe her head dip to the left when she smiled shyly after returning from a night with Nicky; to see it lift up at an angle with a half-smile of slight disbelief when she suspected someone was exaggerating.

Robin had assumed that she was doing the same thing with Tracy. She'd recorded cascading, silky, blonde hair falling back onto broad shoulders as it was released from a clip, the appearance of parallel-lined crinkles at the bridge of her nose as she sat pondering standard deviations. Robin had thought that writing about the minutiae of Tracy's movements was the same kind of observing she did with Angie or Barbara or even Gabi, their RA.

Lately, though, it had become harder to maintain that comparison because what she saw now, what she sought out, were the curves that formed where Tracy's back met her behind, the slight indent above her belly, and the deep, pink warmth that radiated from her chest, exposed when she wore that cream-colored shirt unbuttoned at the top to reveal a hint of her breasts. Robin's words sketched the language of Tracy's soft and round shoulders. She listened past the accent to the timbre of her voice when it dropped below register to a whisper. She wondered in her journal late at night what that whisper would feel like in your ear or on your skin. She wrote at length about how that breath would radiate warmth but also create chills. How sounds produce vibrations, even at a whisper. How full, pink lips must be incredibly soft when they touch your neck.

There was a notebook where all these thoughts were kept. A black and white, mottled, old-fashioned composition notebook, the kind Robin used a lot for writing. This one was hidden at the bottom of a drawer, under sweaters. She usually grabbed it after she and Tracy had spent an afternoon together studying or walking to the nearby shopping center. She had filled pages the night they'd all gone dancing, recording Tracy's arms and legs in motion on the dance floor; the swaying of her hair; the look on her face, a mixture of abandon and cockiness.

Robin thought of the notebook as a parking place where she could get these observations out of her head and into a physical location, relieved that they'd be hidden away at the bottom of a drawer. She always felt unburdened afterward.

Tonight she had recorded a detailed tribute to the ways in which Tracy had handled utensils at dinner; how her long, tapered fingers clutched the knife and gently held the fork; and how she'd lovingly caressed the rounded bottom of a soupspoon, as she listened to Angie detail her plans for ascending the ranks of student government.

As Robin moved to put the notebook away where it would never be seen by anyone else, her phone rang.

"Hello?"

"Robin, it's Joe Donovan, have I called too late?"

"No, I'm awake."

"Good, I wanted to tell you that you're all set with Professor Coolidge for the seminar tomorrow. Are you still sure you want to do this? She's gonna work you like a dog."

"Yeah, Joe, I'm sure. I know it'll be torture but I really need to know this stuff to get deeper into my writing. Coolidge has this ability to get to the heart of things and that's the place I need to get to if I want to write anything worth reading."

"Well, it's your funeral, Robin. The Humanistic Psychology seminar is full of her best psych majors, almost all juniors and seniors. I went to bat for you, but I'm still wondering if I did the right thing. You can always take it sophomore year."

Robin was adamant. "Joe, I need it now. I've got to learn more about motivation and behavior to improve these stories. They aren't there yet."

"Well she agreed to take you, but I have to tell you, she wasn't happy. She makes very few exceptions and I'm worried that she's going to put you through the wringer to make sure you really get how serious this is."

"Joe thanks. Don't worry, I'll handle it. And, oh, I've got two stories I wrote over the break for you to look at next week. They're just first drafts, but I think they're ready for some feedback."

"Robin, what you call first drafts are most people's finished products. I look forward to reading them. Take care and good luck with Professor Coolidge."

#

The classroom was arranged in the traditional format of desks in rows with the teacher at the front. Robin was disappointed, having hoped that a seminar would meet around a large rectangular table or in a circle. She sat down at an empty desk as other students filed into the room. She opened her notebook and reached into her backpack for a pen when she heard a familiar voice addressing her in a whisper.

"Robin, what are you doing in this class?" It was Tracy, standing over her, her voice tense. "This is an upper class seminar."

Robin looked up. "Well then what are you doing here?"

"She makes an exception for her research assistants."

"Well Joe Donovan asked her to make an exception for me, so here I am."

"Why?" asked Tracy, incredulous.

"Would you please sit down?" Robin motioned to the empty desk next to her. "And turn down the attitude. I know it's hard realizing you're not the only teacher's pet."

Tracy sat down and crossed her arms over her chest.

"Look," Robin began, "do you think I'd be here if I didn't need to know this stuff? If I don't understand motivation, how am I ever going to express it in my writing?"

"But why now, while you're only a freshman?"

"I could ask you the same question, princess." She knew Tracy hated the nickname Robin used when she was particularly annoyed.

Tracy breathed out audibly. "If I'm going to be of value to her in her research then I have to understand the area she works in. And it may very well be the area I work in one day."

"Fine. Well if I ever want to write anything that isn't a piece of shit, then I'm going to need this course right now. Otherwise I'm just wasting my time here."

Their exchange was interrupted by the arrival of Professor Coolidge, who spent fifteen minutes outlining the syllabus and the expectations of the class. There were two papers, a project, and a mid-term and final. Joe Donovan hadn't been kidding. It was a killer.

She dismissed the class early after taking questions, which was expected on the first day, and then looked directly at Robin. "Robin, please come see me for a few minutes before you leave."

Tracy gave Robin a questioning look and Robin shrugged her shoulders.

"She's hot for me," she said. "She can't help herself."

Tracy rolled her eyes. "Believe me, she's turned down much better offers."

"We'll see, won't we?"

Robin headed to the front of the room and Professor Coolidge stood to address her, clearly making a point by asserting her superior height of several inches.

"Robin, your presence in this class is nothing more than a favor to Joe Donovan, who happens to be a friend. This is no Psych 101. The level of work is intense and the expectations high. In fact, this is almost a graduate-level course. If you don't take it seriously and deliver good work, then you're out. I'm warning you. Do you understand?"

"Yes" was the strained reply.

"Good. I want to see some samples of your creative writing so I can understand your reasons for taking this course. Joe explained it as much as he could, but I want to hear it from you. So, in addition to the samples, include a one-page written explanation of how the work of this course can improve your creative writing. Are you following me?"

Another "yes" followed.

Professor Coolidge sat down and motioned for Robin to do the same at the nearest desk. Her tone became a little less formal.

"Look Robin, I need you to do something for me. And at this point, you owe me." She paused and looked directly into Robin's eyes. "I want you to stop encouraging Tracy Patterson's pursuit of me."

Robin opened her mouth to say "what?" but Coolidge cut her off.

"I'm not as oblivious as you believe me to be. You think I didn't know what was up with the three of you last semester?" She paused for a few seconds and leaned back in her chair.

"Once every five or six years I come across a student who's incredibly gifted and who needs the kind of mentoring and training that I can provide. Tracy is that student, but I can't do that for her if she has other motives. I've told her that but I don't know if the message was fully received, and it won't be if her friends keep joking and encouraging her. Can you stop that as a favor to me? If you do, I'll call us even and I won't torture you as much as I had planned to." She smiled at Robin.

"Okay, I can do that, if you really mean we're even now."

"Yes, we will be if you follow through. Thank you for agreeing to this."

Feeling dismissed, Robin rose from the desk and started to leave. As she headed for the door, she heard Professor Coolidge's parting words expressed in the clipped, business-like tone she always used as she ended a lecture.

"I'll expect your samples and one-page explanation delivered to my office by the end of the week."

Just as expected, the class was a bear. The reading alone occupied hours of Robin and Tracy's time. They bought one set of books and passed them back and forth, copying pages they both needed to read on the same night. They agreed that the books would be Tracy's to keep, but they would share the cost of a second copy of anything that Robin felt she would want to hold onto after the class was over.

While Robin was barely able to keep up with the demands of the seminar in addition to her other classes, Tracy immersed herself in the subject, reading articles in the *Journal of Humanistic Psychology* that hadn't even been assigned. She breezed through her first paper comparing the discipline of humanistic psychology with that of psychoanalysis and helped Robin with her own paper analyzing the pros and cons of humanistic psychology's focus on individual experience.

"How can this field fully explain human motivation without taking into account the subconscious, the way the Freudians do?" Robin asked one night when she, Tracy, and Angie were together studying.

Tracy looked up and pointed at Robin with her pen. "Don't think of it like it's a religion where you have to choose one belief and reject all the others. Humanistic psychology, psychoanalysis, and behaviorism are separate threads that can be woven together. That's how I think about it."

Robin sat pondering this for a minute. "Hmm, okay, that's helpful. Let me read your paper on psychoanalysis and I'll go back to the book on behaviorism. I think I can come up with a theory about how a focus on individual experience is present in each of them."

Tracy handed Robin the paper she had just printed out.

"Thanks for dragging me through this course," said Robin.

"We're helping each other, you're doing much better with this than I was doing last semester with Jane Austen."

Tracy suddenly jumped up. "Oh shit! I can't believe it. I completely forgot. Hold on I'll be right back." She ran out of the room.

In the time it took for Robin and Angie to look at each other and ask, "What was that about?" Tracy was back, holding a small package wrapped in blue paper with white snowmen.

She thrust the package at Robin. "I'm sorry this is so late. You'll understand why I didn't want to mail it like I did with Angie's gifts. Merry Christmas, I mean, Happy uhhh …"

"Hanukkah?" Angie said.

"Yes, Happy Hanukkah."

Robin looked at both of them and laughed. "It's Chanukah, with a khuh," she said, emphasizing the Yiddish pronunciation with a guttural sound that came from the back of her throat.

"Will you open it?" Tracy asked.

Robin tore through the paper and stared at the three small volumes enclosed in a clear plastic sleeve. Looking quizzically at the cover of the top book, she slid it out and opened to the title page, her eyes wide. She took out the second and the third books, looking closely at each, her breathing audible.

"Robin, what is it?" Angie asked, heading toward her.

Robin looked up, an expression of shock on her face. "It's a first edition copy of *Emma* by Jane Austen," she said with awe and a hint of fear in her voice.

Angie pulled the books out of her hands and regarded them closely, a look identical to Robin's forming on her face.

Finally, Robin turned to Tracy. "How? Where did you get this?"

"Do you like it? I wasn't sure what to get you. You're not so easy to shop for."

Robin stared back at her expecting an answer to her questions.

"I found it at a swap meet near home," Tracy explained to their questioning expressions. "You know, where people come to sell used things on the weekend? This biker couple had no idea what it was. They got it with a bunch of other stuff at an estate sale."

"A-a-are you sure you want me to have this? I mean it's probably worth a fortune."

"Of course, I want you to have it. Don't you want it?"

"Yes, but. I mean this is a big deal. It should, like, be in a museum or something."

"Well, you deserve it; I got an A-minus on that Jane Austen paper last semester."

Robin looked directly at Tracy with a serious but kind expression on her face. Tracy returned the gaze. They remained that way for a long moment, searching for something in each other's eyes, neither of them speaking. Robin could sense Angie reacting to the emotion in the room and saw her look up from the books in her hands and watch the silent intensity of her friends' interaction. But neither of them could look away from the other to include her. Robin stared into Tracy's green eyes feeling frozen in the moment. She was aware of the sound of Tracy's breathing and she felt a hint of something else coming from Tracy. Was it vulnerability?

At last Robin spoke. "Thank you so much. This is incredibly meaningful to me."

"I wanted it to be," Tracy said, still staring.

Finally, not knowing what else to do, Robin looked away and said playfully to Angie. "Hey give me back my books. I won't let you sell them, Antonelli. They're mine. Besides, you don't need the money. You have a full scholarship."

CHAPTER TEN

Professor Coolidge held up eight, bright multi-colored index cards fanned out as if they were a hand dealt to her in a game of gin. She walked around the room identifying pairs of students among the sixteen in the seminar and called out their names, offering a neon-colored card to one member of each pair.

"Tim and Brian."

Brian got a bright green card.

"Charisse and Toni."

Charisse got bright yellow.

"Robin and Tracy."

This was a purple card that Tracy was handed. Robin leaned over to see what it said and was disappointed when all she could read were their two names and in large, handwritten, block letters the word "HAPPINESS."

As Professor Coolidge went about her task, Robin reached over to grab onto a corner of the card, twisting it in Tracy's hands so she could see if there was anything on the other side.

"I checked already. It's blank."

"Well, then, what is this happiness thing all about?"

"I think we're about to find out."

Robin stood to read over Brian's shoulder and saw that his card also had one word on it. It said "FEAR."

Robin turned back to Tracy, pointing to Brian. "His says fear."

Tracy shrugged. "My guess is it's got something to do with Maslow."

"And you would be right, Tracy." It was Professor Coolidge who'd overheard them as she walked back up to the front of the room, her task completed.

"The two members of each of the eight pairs I just assigned will be working together on a project. As you see, the cards I gave you have just one word on them. This word is either a motivator or an end state in the model we've been discussing—Maslow's Hierarchy of Needs.

"The design of your project is completely up to you, with the caveat that it cannot be merely descriptive. I don't want any posters, research papers, or other creative representations of, for example, the need for safety. I want a project that tests the thesis of the theory surrounding your topic word. It doesn't have to be a full-blown experiment, though it could be, but I want you to take some real data or evidence and test the theory. If what you find calls the theory into question, I want you to defend your critique. If your data supports the theory, explain why. Fully describe your methods, including their strengths and weaknesses, consistent with the research design materials we went over early on.

"These projects are due to me on the last day before spring break. That's Friday, March 18. So you have one month to complete them. And yes, I know the mid-term is only a few weeks before and yes, I know you have other classes. But this is where, in our imaginary but not improbable dialogue, I remind you that you chose to take this seminar and you knew on the first day that the work load would be considerable. Now are there any other questions."

As they packed up to leave class, Robin looked at Tracy and said, "Ugh, happiness. How is that ever gonna help me in my writing? Would you be willing to see if Tim and Brian would switch and we could do fear?"

"She'll never let us. I have a feeling all of these assignments were deliberately chosen."

89

As they walked together toward the classroom door, Robin and Tracy were stopped by the familiar voice calling after them.

"Oh, and Robin, switching topics is not permitted."

Robin was quiet until they'd left the building so she could be sure they were out of range. She shook her head back and forth.

"What is with that woman? Does she have bionic ears or something?"

"All seeing. All knowing," said Tracy. "It's scary." She smiled as she steeled herself against the February cold. "I guess we're stuck with happiness.

A week later there was still no clear idea for the project. Robin and Tracy had agreed to read whatever they could get their hands on about Maslow's concept of happiness.

"Let's do something on peak experiences," said Robin. "We can go talk to people who meditate or something and ask them what makes them happy."

"What if we just went around campus and asked students if they're happy and why?"

Robin looked at Tracy and rolled her eyes.

"Permit me to demonstrate why that is a terrible idea," she said and turned toward Angie who was sitting in the opposite corner, trying to read about parliamentary forms of government.

"Angie," Robin asked, "are you happy, and if so, why?"

Angie looked up.

"Right this second, I'm annoyed that you're interrupting me when I'm trying to study. But generally, yes, I'm happy. Why am I happy? Because I have you guys and Nicky."

Robin grinned, and gestured in an exaggerated fashion with her arms, extending them, palms face up, toward Angie and then pivoting to Tracy.

90

"Thank you for proving my point! See, Tracy, you interview college students and all you're gonna get is friends and sex, friends and sex."

Angie looked up and opened her mouth to protest, but then closed it and turned back to her book and pink highlighter.

"I see what you mean," Tracy said. She held her chin in her hand and looked down deep in thought.

"Tracy!" Angie slammed her book down on the desk. "Thanks for agreeing that all I am is shallow and horny."

"Sorry, Angie, I don't think you're shallow."

Robin burst out laughing and Tracy started to giggle.

Angie walked over to the bed where Robin was sitting, put her hands on her shoulders and pushed her down.

"How ironic that it's me who is labeled horny," she said, "when I'm getting more sex than the two of you put together."

"Don't remind me," Tracy and Robin said in unison.

Tracy walked over to the bed and sat down with them.

"No one leaves this room 'til we come up with a project idea."

"I'm not even in this horrible course you're both taking," said Angie

Tracy put her arm around Angie. "You're our best friend, so you're obligated to help us."

"It'll do wonders for your poll numbers, Senator, I promise," Robin said in a hopeful voice.

"All right, let's get this over with," said Angie.

Robin turned to Tracy. "See the poll numbers get her every time."

Angie groaned. "Robin, shut up and think of a project idea before we all die of starvation."

They sat quietly for a few minutes thinking. Robin grabbed her notebook and started scribbling. Tracy looked over her shoulder and saw that Robin had drawn the pyramid-shape of Maslow's hierarchy with an arrow pointing up, but otherwise couldn't figure out what she was writing.

At last, Robin looked up. "Okay, what do you think of this?" she said. "We take your idea and ask our subjects if they're happy and why, but we choose a group that is really struggling to get up the hierarchy of needs because they don't always have enough food or a place to live and they've been rejected by people who were supposed to love them. Then we can test the theory that you need to get through each level of need in order to attain real happiness."

"I like it," said Tracy, "but who are our subjects, people in homeless shelters?"

"Not exactly. They're homeless gay and lesbian kids like the ones I hang out with in the city. But these are Boston kids; every place has them."

The smile on Tracy's face broadened into a grin. "You're brilliant! Coolidge is going to love this!" She threw her arms around Robin, pulling her into a tight hug. Neither of them let go.

As the long hug ended, Robin pulled away with a self-satisfied smile on her face. Tracy picked up one of their shared seminar books and began leafing through it. Angie stood and looked at both of them.

"Well now that you've had your peak experience, guys, can we all go get some dinner?"

#

The three weeks leading up to spring break went by in a blur, much like finals time at the end of the last semester. Tracy and Robin spent every waking moment together studying for midterms and preparing for the project interviews. Tracy had the idea to incorporate Maslow's hierarchy into the design of the project, so they bought subway tokens, warm socks, gloves, and gift cards to give to their interview subjects in order to meet their basic needs and to thank them for their time.

They assured the coordinator at the drop-in center that they wouldn't take too long and would fully explain their project to the kids who participated. Robin brought some of her short stories about life on the streets of New York City to offer to read to the group, even though she still considered them to be first drafts.

The building was in a run down section of Boston's South End, near the city hospital. At Angie's instruction, Robin and Tracy took two subways, the Red and the Orange lines, and walked three blocks carrying boxes of supplies and two mini recorders they'd purchased for the interviews. They entered a tiny lobby, gritty with dirt on the walls, and walked up one flight of stairs to the drop-in center. The blue door they entered had a hand lettered sign that said "BAYS - Boston Alliance of Youth Services." They entered a large open room with old couches and orange plastic chairs and a dark wood table pushed to the side. On the walls were a variety of LGBT history posters featuring Oscar Wilde, James Baldwin, Eleanor Roosevelt, and Gertrude Stein along with safe sex posters and a small photo exhibit of black and white pictures taken at a Gay Pride March.

A tall skinny young man with short auburn hair and an unshaven face came toward them. He smiled and put out his hand.

"Hi, I'm Peter Delany. Are you Robin and Tracy?"

Tracy lay her box down on a plastic chair and put out her hand.

"I'm Tracy and this is Robin."

Robin nodded.

"Great. What did you guys bring us?"

Robin looked around the empty room as Tracy opened the box and started removing its contents.

"Where are the kids?" she asked.

"They'll start trickling in soon," said Peter. "As I told you, we feed them, talk and then let them hang out before we make sure everyone has a place to stay for the night. We have slots set aside for them in some of the local shelters."

The blue door opened and two young boys and a girl entered. One boy was tall and large with short, dark hair and an olive complexion. Robin immediately thought of TJ, a lump forming in her throat. The other boy was African American, thin and wiry with dreadlocks past his shoulders. The girl was white with wavy, light brown hair and a blue baseball cap turned backwards on her head. Robin looked at her and smiled, her eyes wide. The girl smiled back.

Tracy pursed her lips and looked at Robin as more kids entered the room, some in groups, others on their own.

"Behave yourself," she said in an angry whisper speaking into Robin's ear, "this isn't some bar in New York City."

Robin spun toward her in one movement.

"What? All I did was smile at the girl."

"I know that smile and what it means. We're here on a research project, not a pick up project."

"Hey folks." Peter spoke loudly over the din. "Let's get something to eat and then we've got two visitors here with us tonight who are going to ask you for some help with a project they're doing. They brought you cool stuff to share to show their appreciation for your time."

He gestured as he continued, "this is Tracy and this is Robin."

Robin walked over to a small group of boys and one transgender girl still growing out her hair and experimenting with make-up. Tracy headed off to another group. After dinner, everyone assembled in the center of the room sitting in a circle. Robin made an effort to steer clear of the girl with the baseball cap who had been trying to get her attention.

"Okay guys," Peter began, "I'm gonna turn this time over to Tracy and Robin and they'll explain what they're doing."

There were about fifteen kids, mostly boys and a few girls. They slouched in the orange plastic chairs or turned them around and sat hunched over the chair backs.

"Hey, I'm Tracy …"

One of the African American boys interrupted her. "Where you from down South, girl? I'm from Memphis, Tennessee."

"Well, hi," Tracy said with a big smile, her accent a little more pronounced. "I'm from Durham, North Carolina."

He pointed to Robin, "You from there too?"

"No, I'm from New York."

"Ohh," said the girl with the baseball cap. "I knew it. That's where I'm headed soon. Maybe you could give me some pointers."

She smiled seductively at Robin and a chorus of "oooohs" emanated from the boys around her.

"I think the blonde is hotter," another boy ventured.

"But I'm more fun," Robin said to more "ooohs." Tracy's face registered a look of shock and outrage.

"So this is what we want to do with you guys." Robin began again now that all their attention was on her. "We go to school at Adams University, which is up in Somerville, and we're doing an experiment."

"Like with test tubes?"

"No," said Robin, "even more boring than that. It's about happiness."

A few groans and one comment of "why is that boring?"

"You see, there's an old, straight, white guy named Maslow (he's actually dead) but he said that people can't be happy unless they have certain things in their lives. And Tracy and I aren't really so sure about that."

"What kinds of things?" the trans girl asked.

"Like food or a house or good friends," said Tracy.

"I can be happy with two out of three," someone said.

"What kinds of stuff did you bring us?" It was the large boy who'd made Robin think of TJ. "I wanna know if all these questions are worth my time."

"You know," said Robin, "I have this friend in New York City named TJ, and from the minute you walked into this room, you reminded me of her. She would have asked that exact question."

"I remind you of a girl?"

"Hey, TJ is one tough mutha of a butch. No one messes with her. Whenever any of us wanted to take someone we'd met into the bathroom for a little, well you know, fun and games ..." There was knowing laughter and a wolf whistle. "... ol' TJ would stand guard 'til you were all done, which guaranteed that no one would bother you."

Without skipping a beat, Robin went on.

"So we're gonna put you into two groups, one's gonna talk to Tracy and one to me."

"I pick you."

"I want the blonde."

"We're gonna count off," Robin said with authority. "1–2, 1–2."

As they counted, Robin made a mental note of the baseball cap's number and she chose the other group. She and Tracy had a list of identical questions and they spent the next twenty minutes asking the kids to talk about life on the streets and whether they had enough food to eat. When do they feel safe, if ever? They then asked about their families. Do

96

they talk to any of them? Who cared about them? Again and again, they heard about each kid's gay family.

"My gay mother." Usually a gay man. "My lesbian uncle."

"My gay mom bailed me out when they arrested me for leaving the restaurant without paying the check."

"Mine bailed me out when I got pinched for soliciting."

"I stayed with my lesbian uncle and her old lady for a while 'til they got evicted."

When the groups came back together, Robin addressed them again.

"So, you guys, I write these stories about the people I hang out with in New York, like my friend TJ I was telling you about. I thought, if it's okay with you, that I'd read one tonight, and then you'll get the stuff we brought to thank you. Okay?"

"Let's hear the story."

"We'll let you know if it's any good."

"I'm counting on you to do just that," said Robin.

Robin read a story about a tough, young lesbian named Buddy, and her effeminate gay friend, Jerry. The story described an incident where the police harass the two kids after a manager at McDonalds complains that they stayed too long without buying anything. After the police grab the boy and slam him to the ground, the girl tries to run away. She goes down the steps into the subway where she jumps the turnstile and is chased along the platform by a transit cop. As she is cornered at the end of the platform with no visible exit for escape, she begins to relive a similar experience of confinement from her past.

> *Buddy stands with her back against the tiled station wall, its surface encrusted with gray muck, looking from side to side for an exit as the cop grows larger in his approach, his footsteps thudding louder on the concrete.*

It hadn't been that long ago when she'd looked in vain for escape from another dead end. This one in the bedroom of her parents' home where her father and the brother of her former girlfriend had come at her with fists raised, their faces twisted and ugly.

She cowers in the corner, crouching with her back to the wall, steeling herself against the certainty of the blows.

"Filthy dyke, you're disgusting."

"Teach you to lay a hand on my sister."

"You'll wish you were never born."

And when they are there, on her shoulders, her back, a fist to the top of her head.

"Come with us, now!"

She remains crouched against the wall, confused at her surroundings until she is pulled painfully by her left arm to a standing position. Instead of her father and Suzie's brother, there are two uniform cops with batons in their hands pulling her along a subway platform. She has no idea how she's gotten there or why.

The story ends when the boy and girl, reunited on their court dates, are let off with a warning by a gay municipal court judge who sees the situation for what it is. The two kids are remanded into the custody of a gay youth program and told that the charges will be dismissed if they keep their noses clean for ninety days. That night, the boy, Jerry, realizing that the little money he had was stolen from him while in custody, takes twenty dollars from the youth group's petty cash box when someone forgets to lock it. Hearing this, Buddy tells him it's time to leave and to once again go back to life on the streets.

#

As Robin finished reading and looked up, there was silence in the room, except for the sniffling of a few kids. Tracy, who had read the story before, looked down at the floor overcome by sadness.

At last, Peter spoke up in a soft voice.

"Sometimes it's helpful to talk through a story like this one that is so difficult and, I would imagine, so realistic for you guys."

The boy who resembled TJ went first.

"This happened to me. I stayed too long in a restaurant and the cops beat me up."

"I got caught for jumping the turnstiles," someone else said.

In a small voice, the girl with the baseball cap said, "My girlfriend's father attacked me, you know, that way. My parents said I deserved it."

There was a lull in the room that was broken after a minute by the boy from Memphis who said in a loud voice, "You need to keep telling these stories, sister. You need to tell them to the president and the vice president and to the PTA and to the judges. Don't you worry 'bout no school you have to go back to. Just stand outside in the Common with a microphone and tell those stories, again and again."

Everyone around him nodded.

The TJ kid said, "I know I gave you a hard time before. But you're a good writer. Keep at it."

"So let's end with thank you gifts," said Peter as he stood up and walked over to the two boxes sitting on the table against the wall. "What'd you guys bring?"

The kids left their seats and crowded around Robin and Tracy, each of whom had their arms in a box, lifting out socks, gloves, subway tokens, and gift cards. Peter stepped in and organized the distribution process so that it was orderly and fair.

As the kids stood in a clump around Robin and Tracy, the boy with the dreadlocks called out over the other voices.

"Hey, I been meaning to ask. Are you two a couple? Like, are you together?"

"We're friends," Tracy said in a whisper.

The boy persisted. "Not so sure about that, girl. For some reason, I'm feeling more. I think you two like each other. Why don't you kiss and find out?"

Tracy shook her head and began to say, "I don't think…." But she was drowned out by a chorus that began slowly and quickly picked up steam.

"Kiss her! Kiss her! Kiss her!"

Wanting to defuse the situation, Robin leaned over and kissed Tracy on the top of her head. As Robin moved to stand up, Tracy stood with her, leaned over and kissed her full on the lips to a chorus of "Yes!" "Way to go!" "I knew it!"

Robin took a step back and said in a halting voice, "We should get going." Looking away from Tracy, she scanned the faces of the kids and said, "Thank you all so much for your help. We were so happy to meet all of you."

"Y'all are amazing," Tracy said.

"Come back again," someone called out.

"Yes," said Robin. "We will."

Peter shook their hands and thanked them warmly. They walked through the blue door and down the stairs, relieved of the boxes they'd brought with them.

On the walk back to the subway, Tracy rattled on about the interviews she'd taped and the incredible information they had. She wondered if they could debunk Maslow and come up with a new theory about happiness that didn't require a climb up through each level of need. Robin nodded but was silent.

They sat side by side on the Orange Line, not talking over the rustling sound of the train and the frequent stop announcements. At last, Robin nudged Tracy's arm and they looked at one another.

"What was that kiss about?"

"Oh that. I figured they wouldn't stop 'til they got what they wanted."

"That's why I kissed the top of your head."

"Well, you had been the star of the show the whole way through and rightly so. You were great. I have to admit that I could have never been halfway as good as you with those kids. So maybe I wanted to do something dramatic, just to show them that you weren't the only gutsy one."

"So that's all it was? A statement? For the kids?"

Tracy grinned at her. "Let me see that smile again. The one you gave the girl in the baseball cap."

"What?"

"I want you to show me that flirty smile of yours."

"I, I don't know if I can. I mean." Robin sighed and then said, "Okay."

She looked right at Tracy, smiled her lopsided grin and opened her eyes wide.

As they sat looking at one another, she heard Tracy's intake of breath.

"Well now I can see why that little girl wouldn't leave you alone all afternoon. Now, I'm gonna show you mine."

Tracy looked directly at Robin. She tilted her head down at a slight angle and slowly batted her eyes. Her mouth was closed in a kind of half-smile, her green eyes serious and intent.

Robin sat rigid, fixed in place by that look, a feeling of terror and need welling up. She didn't know if she was even capable of looking away.

#

Back on campus Robin begged off dinner to go write. Tracy offered to come by later and bring her something to eat. She had been thinking about a new story she wanted to start. As she sat on her bed with a notebook in her lap, characters introduced themselves in her head, but the idea wasn't gelling. She gave up, thinking it might be better to sit with it for a while and let the plot and character development come to her over the next few days as it usually did.

She was going to dig out the hidden journal at the bottom of her clothes drawer to write about the unexpected and shocking kiss from Tracy, but her mind wandered back to the kids they'd met that day. She picked up her regular journal and began writing about the girl with the baseball cap, the boy with the dreadlocks and the one who reminded her of TJ, especially detailing the way her reading had affected them. Everything the characters in her story had experienced had happened to these kids, not surprising since she always based her stories on what she'd learned from her friends and from the people she'd met at the pier.

She wanted desperately to go back to the drop-in center and do something more for these kids than just bring them warm socks and tales of the hardships they knew only too well. Remembering the boy who had told her to quit school and spend her time broadcasting these stories to the world, she wondered if that's what she should be doing instead of spending four years in an ivory tower learning from famous writers.

Robin thought about Angie's ambition to become a politician and about Tracy's to become a psychologist. Would either of them be able to do something for these kids? What could anyone do so that the father of a young girl didn't think he had the right to brutalize his daughter's female lover? What would it take so that cops didn't think it was acceptable to drag a kid out of a restaurant and beat him senseless? What could she do to make sure Olivia's brother would never touch her again or to prevent a kid's parents from inflicting the kind of pain that leaves a large red welt on the side of her stomach?

Robin thought about her own parents and how easy it had been for her—how they encouraged her writing; how they let her spend her nights in the city; how they made sure she had money, clothes, food, and especially love. She lay on her back, the journal open resting on her chest.

Why her and not TJ? Why Angie and not the girl with the baseball cap? Why did she even have a right to lie on a bed in a room that was hers when those kids got parceled out each night to shelters where they slept head to toe on thin cots? Would it ever matter that she wrote stories about them? Was she co-opting them for her own benefit?

All she had were these questions and her despair. She chastised herself for obsessing about Tracy's kiss when there were kids who had to rely on a stranger to buy them subway tokens so they wouldn't get arrested jumping the turnstiles. She knew that the stuff she and Tracy had brought would last only a couple of days, and then what?

Tears appeared in the outer corners of Robin's eyes and rolled down the sides of her face. Anger and frustration leapt to the surface and she turned her body violently to lie on her stomach, sending the journal and pen flying to the floor. She pounded her fists on the pillow.

"Shit! I'm fucking useless! All of us are useless!"

She buried her face in the pillow and sobbed for the kids and for herself. She felt paralyzed like Buddy at the end of the subway platform, seeing no way out. Her sobs came faster and louder as all of the stories she'd heard surrounded and enveloped her like a knotted ball of wire that was impossible to untangle. As she lay there, crying and chastising herself and everyone she knew for being hopelessly inadequate and ineffective, she was aware of something that felt soft and soothing. She turned her head and saw Tracy, squatting down next to her and rubbing the small of her back, whispering softly in her ear.

"Hey, it's okay. It's okay. Whatever it is, I'm here. Shhh. Shhh. I'm here."

Robin stared at her through her tears and felt the soft tickle of a tissue against her nose.

"C'mon, it's okay. Here, wipe your tears and talk to me. Scoot over."

Tracy nudged Robin to make room on the bed and lay down on her side. She put her arms around Robin's shoulders and drew her close. Robin let herself be held.

"That's right," Tracy encouraged her and held her in silence while Robin calmed down.

"I brought you dinner. Are you hungry?" Her mouth was up against Robin's ear.

Robin still couldn't talk. She shook her head no, and then quickly shrugged her shoulders. She really wasn't sure if she was hungry or not.

Tracy held her close and their bodies fit together in a way that gave Robin a sense of comfort and security, but also fueled her confusion. Did this physical closeness mean something different to Tracy than it did to her?

Robin raised her head from its place on Tracy's shoulder and began to explain in a weak voice.

104

"I was thinking about the kids from today and how hard their lives are and how lucky we've all been compared to them. I couldn't understand why them and not us." She choked back a sob and tried to talk through her tears. "I don't know what to do or what should be done. I feel so powerless to do anything and so useless."

Tracy moved her arms down to Robin's waist and tightened her grip, pulling her closer.

"Oh Robin, if you only knew how much more you're doing than most people. You care so much and you write the most beautiful, heartbreaking stories. One day, I promise you, it will make a difference. Just keep doing it."

Robin held on to her and Tracy rubbed her back and her arms. They stayed like that for a long while until Robin's sadness began to subside and feelings of desire started to take over. She looked into Tracy's eyes searching for a clue. There was intensity and heat at least for a moment until she felt Tracy's body twist off the bed.

"C'mon let's get some food into you. It'll help. We'll keep talking."

Tracy stood and Robin felt a gust of cold air rush in to replace her. She soon followed and walked over to where Tracy was standing at her desk lifting a large flat plate that was covering another plate filled with food. She motioned for Robin to sit down.

"There was lasagna tonight. It's still a little warm."

CHAPTER ELEVEN

In the last week before spring break, the paper for the happiness project practically wrote itself. Tracy drafted the methods section and Robin summarized the data collected. Together, they worked on their theory, its rationale, and how they would modify Maslow's hierarchy. They even settled on a title that they both liked—"On the Rungs In-between: Achieving Happiness on the Way Up the Hierarchy of Needs."

After turning in the project on that last Friday, Robin left for New York. Tracy stayed behind to spend the week with Angie and her family. They'd both been invited to New York the following weekend to attend Robin's family's annual Passover Seder.

Robin was Tracy's first Jewish friend. She'd known a few Jewish kids in high school, but wasn't close to them. Robin didn't usually talk much about religion or about being Jewish, but Tracy remembered a time early on in the fall when they all first became friends. She hadn't seen Robin for most of the day and asked Angie where she was, assuming she was off somewhere writing.

"It's Yom Kippur. She's likely praying and fasting at the services on campus."

"Fasting? Why?"

"Tracy, there must be Jews in North Carolina."

Oh now we're back to this Southerners are stupid thing again, Tracy thought.

"Of course there are, Angie. I just never heard of this…Yom…what is it?"

"Yom Kippur, the Day of Atonement, when Jews ask God to forgive their sins."

"And Robin actually prays all day?"

106

"Seems like it. I saw her leave this morning dressed in her beige blazer, which is about the nicest thing she owns."

Tracy sat down on the bed next to Angie.

"She is full of surprises, isn't she?"

#

Tracy was glad that she'd made the decision to spend the break with Angie. She had no idea what she would have done back in Durham. Brett and Jeff's break was the following week, so they would still be in classes during her visit. Without them to rely on for an escape, she'd be left with just her mother and, given the state of her bitten down nails, that would not have been a good idea.

With Boston weather still cold and wintry in March, Angie and Tracy had to be creative in their efforts to entertain themselves. Harvard had the same week off, but Nicky had gone on a trip with her basketball team. Angie's friend Marla was home from Harvard, so they spent time with her at the movies and going dancing at the women's bar in Boston. They also took two day-trips, one to Northampton and one to Provincetown, which Angie described as "the gayest places in New England."

Walking the icy streets of Northampton, Tracy felt at ease among the college students still hanging around during spring break. The town's funky stores and vegetarian restaurants reminded her of a colder and snowier Chapel Hill. But as she, Angie, and Marla walked along Main Street, she began to notice something she'd never seen back home.

"Look!" she said. "Over there by the bookstore, those two women."

"What about them?" Angie asked, turning her head.

"They're holding hands. In public like that." Tracy then looked to her left. "Wait. Hold on. Look across the street at that coffee place. There's two more."

Angie and Marla looked at each other and began to laugh. "Yes, Tracy, this is Northampton, also known as Lesbianville," Marla said.

"I've never seen ... You could never in North Carolina, not even in Chapel Hill." Tracy opened her mouth, a look of amazement on her face as she spotted two women coming toward them with their arms around each other.

Angie chuckled and jostled Tracy's arm. "If you think this is something, wait 'til we go to Ptown."

The visits to Northampton and Ptown had opened her eyes to a world she didn't think could ever exist, one where gay people could live like anyone else. Angie had taken her to what she called "women's bookstores" but what were in reality lesbian bookstores filled with shelves of novels that told stories about girls falling in love with one another.

As they left one such store in Provincetown, Angie handed Tracy a bag.

"I got you a present."

"Angie, no. I should be getting you a present. You've been so great to me this week."

"Nope. Just look in the bag. But be careful, there's two small things in there that you won't want to lose."

Tracy pulled out a small paperback book. On the cover were two young girls, both really pretty. One had her arm on the other's shoulder. They were looking at each other and smiling. For a quick second she thought of her and Robin.

"Happy Endings Are All Alike."

She turned the book over and read the blurb on the back. It was a love story. She hadn't seen anything like this before.

"This looks great."

She reached back in the bag and pulled out two metal buttons with pins on the back held in place by a small metal piece. She read the first one aloud.

"This is What a Lesbian Looks Like."

Tracy turned to Angie and smiled.

"I like that. I should wear that when I get all dressed up."

Angie grinned at her.

"Read the other one."

"A Woman Without a Man is Like a Fish Without a Bicycle." She paused. "Huh?"

"Exactly," said Angie with a nod of her head.

Tracy looked puzzled.

"Oh wait, I get it. Why would a fish need a bicycle?"

Angie pulled a small button out of her jacket pocket.

"I got this one for Robin."

"Dyke," read Tracy. "Isn't that word, like, offensive?"

"Depends on who's saying it. Robin will wear this as a badge of honor."

"You're probably right."

Tracy began walking, her hands in her pockets and her head down. She smiled to herself thinking of Robin with that provocative button pinned to her dark brown winter jacket. A feeling of warmth and delight enveloped her. She looked over at Angie walking next to her.

"She's gonna love that button."

"I know. Hey, just make sure all this stuff I got you stays in the bag. You've met my mother and you know she's like a bloodhound."

#

"Tracy, do you realize you're pacing?" Angie asked as they hung out in her room the night before they were leaving for New York.

109

"Oh? Am I?" Tracy sat down on the bed. "My friend Jeffy says I'm impatient, but for the life of me, I don't know for what."

Angie gave Tracy one of her disbelieving smiles.

"For someone who wants to be a psychologist, you really have an amazing lack of self-insight."

Tracy opened her mouth to object, but instead looked at Angie with a worried expression.

"Do you think I don't have what it takes to be a psychologist? Maybe I should think about a different major?"

"Oh God, Tracy, Professor Coolidge thinks you walk on water."

"What good is all that research I do for her if I can't even figure myself out?"

"Well, think of it this way. If you have it all figured out when you're nineteen, then what are you going to do with the rest of your life?"

"But you said that for someone who wants to be a psychologist, I have no insight."

Angie put her hands on Tracy's shoulders and looked at her reassuringly.

"And you know what Robin would say if she were here now? She'd say, 'Tracy, why would you ever believe anything a politician says?'"

CHAPTER TWELVE

The Greyhound bus from Boston came into the rear section of the lowest level of New York's seedy Port Authority building. Robin was worried that if she didn't wait right where the bus pulled in, Angie and Tracy would have no idea how to find her. Her father dropped her off at the station, annoyed that he'd have to circle around the congested Times Square area in the car while she waited for the bus to arrive.

As the passengers filed off the bus, Robin had a moment of apprehension when she didn't see Angie and Tracy right away. But then there they were, Angie in her red parka and Tracy in her tan coat with a forest green wool scarf wrapped around her neck.

She hugged Angie and said into her shoulder, "So good to see you."

Then Tracy was in front of her.

"Hey," Tracy said in a soft voice and moved in for a hug.

"Missed you," said Robin into her ear.

"Me too."

Robin put one arm around each of them. "Come, let me lead the two of you out of this disgusting place. Oh, and, welcome to New York City."

Bundled together in the back seat of the car, Robin sat between Angie and Tracy, her father driving and her brother, Adam, sitting next to him up front.

"Where's your mom?" asked Angie.

"She's over at my cousin's apartment helping with the meal. She brought them a seder plate she made in her studio and she's setting it up."

"I read about that," said Tracy, sounding like a student who'd done her homework. "That's the plate with all the symbolic foods, right?"

111

"That's right," said Robin surprised. "Have you been reading Jewish Stuff for Dummies?"

"Well, if you must know," said Tracy, putting her finger on Robin's nose, "I found a book in the Adams library that explained the basics of all the Jewish holidays and then Angie filled me in a little more."

"Angie," said David Greene looking up into the rear view mirror from the driver's seat, "have you been to a seder before?"

"Yes, when my father was the mayor of our city he organized a community seder between the Jewish synagogue, the African American Baptist church, and St. Joseph's, which is our church. We went every year."

Robin gave Angie a mischievous grin.

"Did you tell Tracy the part about how we'll be taking some blood from her to make the matzo?"

Before Angie could respond, Robin's father hit the steering wheel hard with his left hand, a loud thud reverberating in the car. He twisted in his seat to look at his daughter, with an expression of shock and rage on his face.

"Robin, stop that right now! I can't believe you would say something like that! I want you to tell us all what you just described. What is that called?" he asked as he turned back to focus on his driving.

Everyone in the car froze in response to his reaction.

"Dad, I'm sorry. It was just a joke."

"I asked you a question!"

In a very soft voice with her head down, Robin said, "Blood libel."

"What was that? Speak up!"

Lifting her head, her voice filled with embarrassment, Robin replied. "I said blood libel."

"And just what is blood libel, Robin?" her father said.

Robin breathed out audibly realizing she was not going to escape this Socratic lecture.

"It was a lie that anti-Semites spread every Passover. They said Jews killed Christian children to use their blood to make matzo."

"And what happened as a result of the blood libel, Robin?"

"Dad, do we really have to do this? I said I was sorry."

"They killed us," Adam said from the front seat.

David turned his head and looked at his son.

"When we change your name to Robin, you can answer," he said.

His voice was now gentler, but firm. "Just tell us what happened, Robin?"

"Armed bands of Christians went into villages and murdered Jews."

"And who left the Ukraine in 1938 in the dead of winter to avoid another Passover?"

"My grandparents," she said.

Robin leaned forward and put her hands on her father's shoulders. She reached around and hugged him from behind.

"I fucked up, Dad. I really am sorry."

David covered Robin's right hand with his own.

"I know that, Robbie. It's okay. Everyone makes mistakes. Don't worry, but just don't do it again. I still love you, you know."

"I love you too, Dad."

"Now sit back and help me look for parking."

Robin slid back between Angie and Tracy. Angie squeezed her forearm quickly and Tracy took Robin's hand in her own.

"You okay?" she whispered in Robin's ear.

Robin nodded and looked down in amazement to see their fingers intertwined. Every cell in her body felt warm and filled with electricity. Tracy looked straight ahead, a slight smile on her face. A few minutes later,

113

as the car moved backwards into a spot on the street and then pulled forward to a stop, Tracy reached for the door handle and turned to get out. In that moment, she pulled her hand free. Robin felt the loss. It was like a switch had been flipped from on to off.

The Greene family's seder commemorating the ancient Hebrew slaves' escape from Egypt was raucous and fun, filled with singing and laughter and memories of past seders when Robin and Adam were younger. Every person was expected to read passages from copies of the book they used to follow along with the ritual and to tell the story of persecution and salvation. Tracy sat between Robin and Angie and was able to get the benefit of their help pronouncing words and names that were unfamiliar.

As the pre-dinner portion of the seder drew to a close, each of them was instructed to prepare what the book described as a Hillel sandwich— two small pieces of matzo substituting for bread, with a layer of strong horseradish and a prepared sweet mixture of apples, nuts, honey, and wine inside.

"This reminds us that in life we need to take the bitter with the sweet," Robin said.

Robin prepared a Hillel sandwich for Tracy and held it to her mouth. As a small amount of the mixture began to escape from between the rigid squares of matzo, Tracy tried to catch it with her tongue and instead licked Robin's fingers, her tongue lingering a few seconds longer. Their eyes locked with the intimacy of the touch and Robin noticed that Tracy's breathing had quickened. Tracy blushed, took the sandwich from Robin's hand, and popped it into her mouth.

With the final chorus of the last song, the seder ended at around ten o'clock. Wendy, David and Adam headed back home to Long Island while Robin, Tracy, and Angie took advantage of a Saturday night in Manhattan to go down to the Village and meet up with Robin's friends.

114

"C'mon, your subway chariot awaits," said Robin as she ushered them out of the apartment door.

"We're takin' the subway this late at night? Isn't that dangerous?" asked Tracy.

"Not with me along to protect you."

The tall, thin woman with the long ponytail at the door of The Well quickly glanced at their fake IDs, took their ten-dollar cover and let them in. The place was small and dark with a dull, wooden bar and a few tall stools to the right. Rickety round tables and chairs painted black were arranged haphazardly on the left. A red, velvet curtain straight ahead led to the dance floor, the sound of the music within radiating to the front. The place smelled of smoke and stale beer.

Robin scanned the room and quickly found TJ, Sophia, and Olivia at a table near the back. They'd arrived hours ago to avoid the cover.

"Robbie!"

Sophia grabbed her into a tight hug.

"Hey, how's my girl Sophia?"

"Missing my friend Robbie, that's how."

Robin grabbed hold of Sophia's ample hips and relaxed into the hug. Sophia wrapped her chubby arms tight around Robin. They stood there holding on to each other.

"Okay, break up this touching scene and let me say hello to my little buddy."

It was TJ towering over them.

"Yo, Teej."

Robin moved to shake hands and instead found herself lifted up by her waist to TJ's full height. They looked at each other eye-to-eye and grinned. Robin heard Tracy and Angie laughing behind her.

"Okay, put me down so I can introduce you."

115

TJ eased Robin onto the floor.

As they all got acquainted, Angie went to buy the first round of drinks.

Robin walked TJ back toward the door.

"What's Olivia doing here?" she asked.

"It's cool," said TJ, "she's not lusting after you anymore."

Robin nodded, relieved.

"Are you and she…?" she asked pointing to TJ, knowing she didn't have to finish the question.

"Now and then," she said, "you know how it is. She's a cutie. And now she knows how to keep that perv of a brother away."

Walking back toward the table, TJ leaned over and pointed her head in Angie's direction. "That one with the dark hair is pretty hot."

Robin shook her head. "Off limits, she's got somebody. Plus she only dates jocks."

"Jocks! Really? How come? Is that some kind of sickness?"

Robin bent over laughing. "Yes, I think so," she said.

"So where is this mystery person of hers?"

"She's off on a spring break trip with her basketball team."

"Oh, a real Romeo, huh? She leaves that cute little girl all by herself in the big city?"

"To tell you the truth," Robin said, "Tracy and I are not so crazy about Nicky. She's got Angie wrapped around her finger and she knows it. But Angie is head over heels. There's no talking to her."

"Tracy and I, huh? What's that all about?" TJ asked.

Robin shrugged. TJ responded silently with a look that communicated skepticism, her eyebrows raised, head tilted.

Tracy sat chatting with Sophia and Olivia. They were all talking and smiling, clearly enjoying themselves. Robin, TJ, and Angie moved their

116

chairs over while Olivia was telling a story about a summer she had spent as a child visiting her grandmother in North Carolina. Tracy seemed happy to be talking about the South and was especially animated when Olivia and Sophia asked her about life in Durham.

Robin was intrigued by the mixed feelings Tracy seemed to have about her home. On the one hand she had been thrilled to avoid a trip back there over spring break. But now in this conversation, she looked so comfortable and happy talking about her life in high school picking up older women in Durham's lesbian bars.

While Robin was glad that Tracy was getting along with her friends, she had to admit that hearing Tracy's fond memories of former exploits made her a little uncomfortable. *It's not like I sit around telling people about my own sexual adventures*, she thought, and almost immediately had to laugh at herself. Here was Olivia, living proof of Robin's past, sitting right next to Tracy.

After sitting awhile, Robin noticed Tracy beginning to move to the beat of the music coming from the back room. The DJ was playing "I Like to Move It," a song that screamed "dance!" with its funky beat and reggae-inspired rhythms. Tracy stood up and made an upward motion with both hands.

"C'mon y'all, there's no way anyone should not be dancing to this song."

Once on the dance floor, they remained in their little group, though TJ maneuvered herself near Angie, who was nice as always but not especially encouraging.

The music faded right into the next song. Jody Watley's "Your Love Keeps Working on Me," slowed the tempo a bit, but its steady R & B beat was still fast enough to keep them dancing in a group. About a minute into the song, Robin and Tracy drifted toward one another and began to dance together, their bodies mirroring each other's movements in a back and forth motion, as they stood smiling at one another. Their hands met and they continued dancing, very much connected through their fingers, the beat of the music, and the intensity of their gaze.

I don't know what you do to me

When I think about you, yeah, it sets me free

After the last repeated chorus faded, there was a quick silence until they heard a familiar organ note that began as a faint sound and slowly became louder. As the opening of Sara McLachlan's "Possession" became apparent to them, a look of surprise and delight shone of Tracy's face and she moved toward Robin for the slow dance.

"I love this song," she said into Robin's ear.

"Me too, I'm wearing out the CD."

Tracy moved her hands to Robin's shoulders. Robin put hers on Tracy's waist. They looked directly at each other, singing the lyrics they each knew by heart.

…would I spend forever here and not be satisfied?

During the musical bridge, Tracy laid her head on Robin's shoulder and moved closer. They swayed together to the music, almost standing in place. Robin sang the next verse into Tracy's ear.

Once again Tracy raised her head to sing the chorus with Robin while holding on tight. As the final strains of music died down into silence, Robin moved her head forward and kissed Tracy. It was not tentative. It was not questioning. It was a kiss that communicated all the feelings and intensity of that moment. Her lips pressed firmly onto Tracy's; her hand caressed soft, blonde hair. Tracy willingly accepted the kiss and when it ended Robin felt Tracy move in for a second kiss, also deep and unflinching.

Robin felt like her whole life clicked into place. She had been wishing, hoping that this was where they were headed. All those longing looks, all the reassuring touches, and the hugs that lasted a few seconds too long to just be called friendly. Robin opened her mouth to begin exploring Tracy's soft lips with her tongue. Tracy's lips parted for her, but as soon as she touched the soft place inside, she was jarred by Tracy suddenly pulling away and taking a step back. Robin's eyes flew open and she stood gaping in surprise, as Tracy, now a few feet away, was shaking her head no. She raised her hands to her mouth and said, "I'm not... It's not.... I can't. I can't."

For a moment, Robin was rooted to the spot unable to understand what was happening. It was as if someone had violently grabbed the arm of a record player and screeched the needle across an album leaving a deep and painful gash on the vinyl surface. As she watched Tracy and felt the now empty space around her, a tight lump formed in her stomach threatening to erupt upward like a volcano.

She spun around and darted in the direction of the bathroom, jumping the line and bolting through the door. As she ran into the brightly lit room, a woman was leaving one of the three stalls. She rushed by her into the now empty toilet, dropped to her knees and lowered her head into the oval opening just in time as her entire dinner came up. She grabbed on to the white porcelain while her body shook violently and tears began to sting her eyes. Another wave soon hit and she was again at the mercy of her body. She held on tight, her knees starting to ache on the tiled surface of the floor.

"Robbie, Robbie, are you okay?"

It was Sophia on the other side of the stall just as Robin's stomach gave way once more.

"Oh my God, Robbie, let me help you."

119

"Sophia, I can't talk. Go away, please," Robin said, her voice shaking.

It was another few minutes of heaving nothing and tears flowing before Robin could get up off her knees and leave the stall. She opened the door and saw TJ standing at the sink wearing her large, navy parka with Robin's brown jacket folded over her right arm. Her broad, olive-toned face held an expression of seriousness and concern. She spoke softly with a hand on Robin's shoulder.

"Wash your face and come with me."

As Robin ran water into her cupped hands and splashed it onto her face, TJ was ready with white paper towels. She gave Robin her jacket and led her out of the bathroom.

Draping her large arm around Robin's shoulder, she said, "I want you to walk with me to the door. Look straight ahead and not at anybody. Just walk with me."

They moved toward the exit, the tall broad TJ and her diminutive friend looking even smaller than usual all hunched over and defeated. Once outside, they huddled against the cold, two doors down from the bar.

"Greene, do you remember our pact from last summer?"

Robin blinked in confusion and shook her head slightly.

"You know, after the Jersey girl, the one with the long dark hair, the dark brown eyes, and the killer body. Do you remember what she did?"

"She dumped you," Robin said feeling dazed and muddled.

"Yeah, and *you* were right there to pick up the pieces, though I have to admit, I was never classy enough to lose my dinner in the bathroom." TJ smiled and grabbed onto Robin's shoulders, shaking them playfully.

"And afterwards," she said, "we made the pact."

"Right." Robin nodded her head. "No more princesses."

"Do you remember what we said? Why we decided no more princesses?"

Robin responded in a small voice. "Because they reel you in and then throw you back."

"Yup. And so we make that pact and you go off to that school and who do you bring back? The princess of all princesses. Princess Di and Princess Leia all rolled into one. A blonde version of that one from, you know, the movie with Clark Gable about the South."

"Scarlett O'Hara."

"That's the one! A blonde Scarlett O'Hara."

"She's not…"

"Oh, Greene, don't go defending the girl when she's already thrown you back. No way. I think you just forgot. You went up to that school and, you know, you got a little soft around the edges."

TJ put her hand on Robin's stomach.

"It's okay though. Because, little buddy, I'm here to toughen you back up. Now, you gotta just keep moving forward right past this girl. Pack her in and don't look back. Just like you told me with Miss New Jersey, right? You go play around with someone else and you don't give her a second thought."

TJ hoisted Robin by her waist and lifted her a foot up off the ground.

"Okay, now try and get down."

"Teej…" Robin began pleading. She was still weak and dizzy from her time in the bathroom and was sure she couldn't muster the strength to free herself from TJ's grasp.

"C'mon, struggle. Push against me! Fight me so you can get back down there."

There seemed to be no way to get out of this. Resigned to the challenge, Robin twisted her body trying to escape from the firm grip on her sides. She pushed hard onto TJ's chest with her hands and rocked herself back and forth. She kicked her feet in the air and finally reached to gain leverage by pressing against TJ's thighs with the soles of her shoes. At last, she felt her friend's grip loosen in the struggle and she was able to drop down to a standing position.

Robin looked up at TJ and smiled. Somehow, this little tussle had restored some small amount of confidence. TJ smiled back satisfied.

"That's more like it. Now, you gonna do it? You gonna move right past her?"

Robin nodded. "Yeah. The princess pact is back in force."

"Yes it is, Greene."

#

On the train ride back, the three of them were silent. The railroad car was almost empty and the awkwardness of the situation led them to sit in separate rows. As they left the last stop in New York City on their way to Long Island, Tracy walked over to where Robin was sitting and took the seat right next to her. Ignoring her, Robin looked out the window into darkness.

"Robin, I'm sorry," she said.

Robin turned away from the window but refused to look at Tracy. With her eyes focused on the seat in front of her, she asked, "What are you sorry for?"

"I'm sorry I hurt you."

Robin shrugged with her eyes still facing forward. "It's not a big deal. I'm over it."

Tracy looked at Robin staring straight ahead with a blank expression on her face.

122

"Can things go back to the way they were then? You know, before this?"

"Sure," Robin said, drawing her feet up onto the edge of the seat and resting her arms on her knees. "I'm thinking they'll be even better."

Robin reached into her jacket pocket and drew out a paperback copy of Dostoevsky's *Notes from Underground* and began to read. Tracy got up and walked back to where she'd been sitting. Robin looked up from her book and noticed Angie watching the two of them, a look of concern and what could only be described as dread on her face.

CHAPTER THIRTEEN

Professor Coolidge stood at the front of the seminar class holding a stack of papers, a mischievous smile on her face.

"Where are my seniors in this class?" she called out.

About eight students raised their hands.

"And the juniors?"

Five more hands went up.

"You people are about to get your behinds kicked by two lowly freshmen."

A few heads turned toward Robin and Tracy who sat in their usual seats, side by side, but slightly turned away from one another.

Dressed in her standard wool blazer and matching neatly pressed pants, Professor Coolidge stood directly in front of them and looked down smiling. She lowered something onto Tracy's desk, which she recognized immediately as their project paper.

"Congratulations Tracy and Robin," Professor Coolidge said, "highest project grade in the class and well deserved."

Tracy looked down at the paper's title page and saw the Professor's now familiar handwriting in blue ink: "A+ excellent research and analysis." Below it were her comments:

This is a sophisticated and nuanced analysis based on a small but significant sample of data from a population that should be laboring in the lower rungs of the hierarchy but has, despite the odds, achieved a measure of happiness. You approached your research knowledgably and sensitively, tested established principles against it and constructed a counter-theory based on your data that is a formidable challenge to the prevailing orthodoxy. Well done! Happiness indeed!

Tracy leafed through the pages, reading the shorter comments and questions throughout. She glanced over at Robin who sat looking down at her notebook, her body still turned slightly away. Tracy passed the paper over and said, "A-plus," with a smile. "This is unheard of from her."

Robin nodded, glanced at the title page, passed the paper back and stood to leave, mumbling, "Happiness indeed" as she rose from her seat. Tracy watched her and noticed Professor Coolidge's questioning eyes following her through the doorway.

#

Tracy was spending more and more time in the library in an out-of-the-way place called the Miles-French Room. Outfitted with dark wood tables and chairs; comfortably cushioned, upholstered armchairs with flowery patterns; and dark rose carpeting, Miles-French reminded her of Victorian-era drawing rooms she had read about in old British novels. Bookshelves lined the walls and long drapes with gold, red, and green designs hung from the high windows. The cozy room could accommodate only about twenty students, so it was usually quiet and removed from the noisy reserve desk where most people congregated.

She had stumbled upon the place one day trying to make her way back from the lower stacks where she had gone to do some research for Professor Coolidge. She walked up an unfamiliar staircase thinking it would get her back to the Reserve Room, but instead it sent her to the rear part of the library building. Curious at the sight of a set of dark wooden double doors, she opened one and peered inside catching her first glimpse of a place that seemed almost magical and out of step with the otherwise modern, light-wood décor of the rest of the library.

Tracy spent hours in the Miles-French Room, reading while curled up in a soft armchair or taking notes at a table. She brought her new IBM laptop there and wrote her papers. It was a peaceful place, and most important, it was removed from the people in her classes and on her hall, including one person in particular.

She'd needed a new refuge now that Robin had become so distant, and now that Robin's room was no longer the home base it had once been. In fact, Robin was hardly ever around. Angie said she was often in Boston at the BAYS drop-in center, where she was running a writing group for the homeless kids and teaching them how to tell their own stories.

Tracy buried herself in her schoolwork and her research job. After asking Professor Coolidge for extra projects in one of their weekly meetings, the professor stated that she could not see how Tracy could be so prolific in completing these projects while carrying a full course load that included the demanding seminar.

"Are you afraid that the quality of the work I do for you will suffer if I take on more?" Tracy asked with concern.

"No, everything you give me is flawless, always on time, and always thorough. I just don't know how you manage it all."

"Easy," she had replied. "I have no life."

As the weather improved in April, Tracy was able to be outside more often, taking regular three-mile walks alone from Adams to Harvard Square, where she absentmindedly window shopped and spent hours in the Harvard Coop looking at books and CDs. She found an ad on a bulletin board at a café for a modern dance class at a studio that was another mile-and-a-half walk further, and signed up.

A few times a week she and Angie made sure they had dinner together since Angie spent a lot of time off-campus with Nicky or at student government meetings on campus. When their conversations became stilted and polite, Angie would look at Tracy and shake her head. Tracy would just quietly eat her dinner and continue to ask Angie about her classes, or Nicky, or the student Senate.

126

One night as they walked back to their dorm after one such dinner, Angie pulled Tracy off the path on the quad and led her by the hand down a grass-covered hill where she motioned for them to sit down.

"What is it?" Tracy asked as she turned to Angie, who sat with her legs extended straight ahead, her hands resting on the grass behind her.

"If you look over there," Angie said, motioning with her chin to an expanse of trees, "you'll see an elephant. A great big, gray elephant, with a trunk and a tail, the whole deal."

Tracy looked at the trees and then at Angie, thinking maybe she was hearing her wrong.

"That elephant has been following us around for a while," Angie said. "It never says anything; just sits there watching us eat dinner."

"Angie, I…"

"Yeah," she said, ignoring Tracy, "that is your proverbial 'elephant in the room,' the thing that's always there that we never talk about. Don't you think it's time that we do?"

Tracy sat cross-legged and looked down at the grass, pulling up a few blades from the dark brown earth. Her blonde hair fell forward obscuring most of her face.

"There's nothing to talk about really," she said and suddenly felt an overwhelming sadness.

"Everything is different and there's nothing to talk about? Hard to believe," Angie said. "Why don't we just start with how you're feeling?"

"I'm not feeling anything. I'm just working."

Angie turned to fully face Tracy. "Have you talked to her?"

"No. She's never around and when she is she ignores me." Tracy's sadness had transformed into irritation.

"Tracy, what happened that night in New York? Why did you stop things?"

In a quiet voice that was almost a whisper, Tracy said, "I don't know."

"Were you scared?"

Tracy stood up, put her hands on her hips and sighed.

"Angie, I know you want to help. But I can't do this. I just need to get through the semester."

Angie stood and took Tracy's hand.

"Wait. It's been so awful watching the two of you. I just wish you could talk it through with one another."

"Angie, I'm not sure you can fix this. I'm not sure any of us can." Tracy's voice was gentle but firm.

"Well, what about the plan I discussed with you? Are you still gonna be around Saturday night when Nicky comes over with her friend from New York? Robin said she'd be there and maybe you could see if she'll talk."

They began walking back up the hill in the direction of their dorm.

"I said I'd be there so I could meet Nicky's friend," Tracy said. "I'm doing this just for you. I can't make any other promises about what will happen."

They paused and Angie opened the glass door of the dorm building and let Tracy go through first. Tracy turned back to her.

"Oh, and, what's this person's name again?"

"Murph," Angie said.

"What kind of name is that?" Tracy asked.

"A jock name I guess. She plays basketball with Nicky in New York."

Tracy rolled her eyes. "Sounds great. Can't hardly wait," she said.

CHAPTER FOURTEEN

Tracy walked down the hall and into Angie's room, a space that still mostly reflected her roommate who was away for the weekend visiting her boyfriend. On the walls were the girl's high school pennants, her cheerleading photos, and poster-sized pictures of her boyfriend in his hockey gear. Angie had claimed only the small piece of wall above her desk on which she had hung her Sweet Honey in the Rock poster and an old sign from her father's campaign for mayor of Medford; the name, Antonelli, was prominent in large red block letters.

Angie and Robin were sitting on the bed, so Tracy walked over to Angie's desk and sat in her chair. Before she could say anything, Nicky burst in with a tall, lanky Murph behind her. A good four inches taller than Nicky with stick straight dirty blonde hair that went past the nape of her neck but above her shoulders, Murph strode in carrying a basketball.

Nicky was wearing a worn denim jacket over her sleeveless John Lennon NYC t-shirt, white with black lettering and a black stripe around the collar. Murph had on a dark blue New York Knicks t-shirt with a picture of a basketball prominently displayed.

Angie got up off the bed and went to Nicky who drew her into a hug and kissed her.

"Hi baby," she said, "meet my pal, Murph."

Murph gave Angie a kiss on the cheek and then turned back to Nicky.

"Didn't do too bad for yourself, I see."

Nicky grinned. "Nope."

Tracy grew exasperated by this whole display. She remembered countless conversations she and Robin had had about how Angie followed

Nicky around like a puppy dog. Tonight was one of the few times that Nicky had come out to Adams. Usually Angie always went to Harvard. During snowstorms, with ice on the road, in single-digit temperatures and during the pressure of finals, Nicky never came to Angie. *So much for lesbian relationships being equal,* Tracy muttered to herself. *Ugh, what does Angie see in Nicky? And now, who is this Murph creature that she's brought with her?*

"Murph," Nicky said, her hand extended first in front of her and then to the side, "this is Tracy and this is Robin."

Murph walked over toward Tracy who said a quick hello and then immediately got interested in something on Angie's desk.

Placing the basketball in front of her, holding onto the opposite edge of the desk and leaning forward toward Tracy, Murph whistled a tone that signaled, "wow." Tracy looked up, saw a disheveled, boorish, and smug person, a taller version of Nicky, and thought to herself, *not if you were the last woman on earth.* She smiled slightly and shook her head no.

"Not happening," she said and picked up one of Angie's books, suddenly interested in macroeconomics.

"Your loss, ice queen," Murph said and spun around tossing the basketball to Nicky who caught it before it could hit Angie in the head.

Tracy looked up again and caught a glimpse of Robin's flirty smile directed at Murph.

Oh, she's not. She couldn't be, she thought.

"And you're Robin, right?"

"That's me," said Robin who was sitting on Angie's bed with her back against the wall.

Murph jumped onto the bed and sat beside Robin, both their legs extended across the width of the mattress, Murph's feet hanging off the edge.

"You're cute," said Murph, who was rewarded once again with the smile.

Desperate for a distraction, Tracy looked toward Nicky and drew her into a conversation, asking about her classes, her basketball season, her plans for the summer, anything to avoid hearing what Robin and Murph were discussing in quiet tones on the bed, their heads way too close to one another. She glanced over again and saw that Murph's arm was now behind Robin's head with a hand resting on her shoulder. Robin grinned and laughed a little, poking Murph playfully in the stomach. A wave of dizziness came over Tracy and she grabbed on to the handle of Angie's desk drawer trying not to watch.

Unable to disguise her sense of dread any longer, she gave Angie a pleading look, wanting her to help in some way that she couldn't describe. Angie took notice and responded discreetly with both palms up, a gesture that indicated she didn't know what to do. Tracy followed Angie's gaze over to the bed where Murph and Robin were now kissing. Murph's hands were all over Robin, moving up and down her arms and reaching lower.

Instantly Tracy felt her world come apart. Exposed in that moment, everything she'd been keeping at bay suddenly came rushing to the surface and anger rose from a place deep inside her.

How could this be happening? How could she be kissing Robin? How could Robin do this in front of me?

She couldn't remember a time when she'd ever been this furious. She wanted to stand up and pull them apart. *Get your hands off her! How dare you?*

She had to leave but she had no idea how.

Instead it was Murph who got up off the bed, asking for directions to the bathroom. Nicky opened the door.

"C'mon I'll show you. It's down the hall."

Tracy rose from the desk chair and looked directly at Robin who was still sitting on the bed.

She walked over, anger clear on her face and in her voice.

"I hope you know what you're doing," she said, her voice shaking.

Robin looked back at her, her eyes wide and serious.

"Actually I do. And what does it matter to you?"

Tracy breathed in audibly and stared. Then she said the meanest thing she could think of.

"I would suggest you take care not to catch any diseases tonight."

Robin moved off the bed and stood only inches from Tracy.

"You know, that was a really fucked up thing to say, even for you."

Tracy turned and walked out, mumbling a quick goodbye to Angie.

She kept walking—down the hall, out of the building and off campus. She hurried down the busy streets along Massachusetts Avenue, trying to burn off her anger. Passing up the straight bars in Harvard Square, she knew that spending hours getting hit on by guys would only make an awful night worse. So she continued further along, until she found herself in grittier Central Square, where there was a small gay bar near MIT. As she entered the bar and paid the five-dollar cover, she was still seething.

"You do know this is a gay bar?" the large bearded man at the door asked her.

Tracy angrily pulled something out of her pocket and showed it to him. It was the button that Angie had bought her in Ptown—"This is what a lesbian looks like." He smiled and ushered her inside with a flourish of his arms.

She didn't bother to look around the place and just sat at the bar with her head down, ordering a vodka and cranberry juice, which she drank quickly and then asked for another, trying unsuccessfully to get the picture of Robin and Murph out of her head.

Nothing made sense. How had she and Robin gotten to this point where they were barely speaking? Did Robin hate her? What did she even want with Robin? Well, for one thing, she didn't want to watch her getting kissed by someone else. And she didn't like the idea of someone else's hands all over Robin.

She looked for the bartender so she could order another drink and noticed a rather large man sitting on the stool next to her. His bulk was precariously balanced on the small seat and his wavy light brown hair could have benefitted from a few minutes of combing. He turned his head and looked at her and she saw a clean-shaven face, pale skin, and soft brown eyes.

"Rough night?" he asked and pointed to her drink. "You either have a roaring urinary tract infection and have to drink a lot of cranberry juice or someone done you wrong."

"I'd feel better if all I had to worry about was an infection."

"Hmm. Boy trouble or girl trouble?"

For the second time that night, she pulled out the button.

He smiled. "Interesting calling card."

"I'm sick of answering the question," she said with resignation.

"Not sick enough to cut off all your hair and put on a flannel shirt, I bet?"

"If that includes having to give up reading *Vogue* then all bets are off." She smiled at him.

"I'm glad to hear there's some lines you just won't cross." He returned the smile and put out his hand. "Hey, I'm Charlie, by the way."

"Tracy, by the way." She shook his hand and pointed to the pink liquid in the glass in front of him. "What's that you're drinking?"

"A Cosmo. Want one? I'm buying this next round."

"Why not? It's pink after all. I wouldn't want to start drinking beer. It might ruin my girly image."

He caught the eye of the bartender, pointed to his drink and put up two fingers.

"You're not from around here, are you?" he asked.

"Yes and no. I'm from North Carolina but I go to school at Adams. What about you?"

"Southie born and bred. Um, that's South Boston for the uninitiated. You probably hear the accent right? It's especially strong when I have to pahk the cah…"

They both spoke at once. "….in Hahvad Yahd." They laughed and clinked their glasses together.

"Yes, an oldie but goodie," he said with a sigh. "So who did you wrong sweetheart? I have ties to the Irish mafia."

"Oh, I don't want her killed by someone else. I want to murder her with my own two hands. Ugh," she said with waving off the topic, "I'm having such a good time talking to you; it would be a pity for us to have to wallow in the depths of my despair. Tell me about yourself instead."

He took out his wallet and handed the bartender a twenty-dollar bill to pay for their drinks. Then he leaned in close to Tracy and whispered.

"By day, I'm a lowly assistant manager in the women's department at Filene's, but at night I'm an empress of the Imperial Court."

"Is that so, Your Highness?" she said with a small smile.

"I'm getting the distinct impression that you don't believe me."

Tracy took a generous sip of her new drink.

"Yum, this pink drink is wonderful. One more of these and you'll be able to convince me that you're Tinker Bell."

"Well, I do believe in fairies. Don't you? But actually, I *am* the empress of the Imperial Court of Boston. We're an organization that raises

134

money for local gay groups. We have chapters all over the country. Here, let me show you."

He took out his wallet again and flipped through the plastic inserts that held credit cards and IDs until he came to a photo that he lifted up for her to see.

Tracy looked at the picture and then at Charlie and then back at the picture. She saw a rather large woman with a lot of make up, her reddish hair piled high on her head, topped off by a very prominent tiara. Her dress was gold lamé with a low neckline. There was something vaguely familiar about her face.

She continued to stare at the picture and then opened her mouth in astonishment.

"Oh my God, this is you!"

"In the flesh. Empress Sheena Tayknoguff at your service."

Tracy hesitated a moment and then laughed. "She no take no guff?"

"I wanted it to be take-no-shit but the Court said absolutely not. So we compromised."

He motioned to the bartender for two more drinks.

"Oh, I'd better not," Tracy said, touching him on the arm.

"Don't worry. What kind of empress would I be if I made you go home to Adams on your own. I'll drive you back up there. But I still want the she-done-you-wrong story."

"Well then I'd better have that next drink."

"You know, you should come to one of our Court events. I think you'd appreciate the pageantry. We actually have some biological women among our ranks."

"If there's a tiara in it for me, I just might."

Their drinks came and Tracy put her money down. "My turn, Your Highness."

"Well, now," said Charlie, "I'll have to go to confession for taking financial advantage of a poor college student."

"If that's the worst thing you have to confess, you're doing pretty well for yourself," Tracy said as she lifted her glass to him.

He leaned over to get closer. "Then I might as well spill the beans and tell you a very horrible secret about me. That *would* be the worst thing I'd have to confess, if I ever dragged my sorry ass back into a Catholic church, that is. I basically live like a nun."

"Do empresses have to take a vow of chastity?"

He laughed. "No, but in my case it just comes naturally."

Tracy looked down at her drink and spoke to it. "I had to sit and watch her kissing someone else. Someone totally loathsome."

Charlie put his hand on her arm and looked at her seriously, his eyes full of sympathy. "Better loathsome than awesome, don't you think? It's a lot easier when you can hate them."

"I'm so angry at her, I walked all the way from Adams to here and I still couldn't calm myself down."

"And that's why God made the Cosmo dearie," he said, lifting his glass and downing the rest of his drink.

"Amen to that," she said and did the same thing.

On the drive back to campus, Charlie gave Tracy his phone number and then serenaded her with a chorus of "You've Got A Friend."

"So you gonna be able to forget about this girl? Maybe find a nice Southern girl, like…"

"Charlie, if you say the names Scarlett O'Hara or Blanche Dubois I'm going to make you let me off right here."

He turned his head from the road and looked at her dramatically as if she had insulted him.

"Do you think I would traffic in such horrible clichés? I am deeply offended." He put his hand to his heart. "I was going to say Reese Witherspoon, that new young actress who's getting a lot of attention."

"She is cute, but I seem to be a little stuck at the moment." She turned to face him and sighed. "It's all such a mess. There's only a couple of weeks left to the semester and then I'll be back in Durham for the summer."

"Then what?"

"Then I have to contend with my momma."

"Are you gonna show her that button you showed me?"

"Not quite yet. Momma still hasn't gotten over the fact that I bite my nails. I'm not sure she's ready to deal with her blonde-haired, little girly girl liking other girls. This is the kind of thing one doesn't discuss in polite company in the South."

"Ohhh," he said turning to her as he waved his arm in a dramatic gesture, "*You* can say that, but *I'm* still forbidden to mention Scarlett or Blanche?"

"Well, okay then, fair is fair," she said with mock seriousness. "How about we compromise with *Steel Magnolias*? I will let you indulge your need to stereotype by using that movie as a reference point."

He giggled.

"So what's she-done-you-wrong like? What makes her so special?"

Tracy let out a groan. "I wish I knew. Half the time I want to throttle her." She paused and then continued. "But actually, she's incredible—brilliant, cute, funny, fearless, and an amazingly talented writer."

"Ooh, the creative ones are not so easy to shake. I once fell for an actor."

"I'm sure you did," Tracy said.

"Hey, now who's trafficking in clichés?" he said. "However accurate they may be."

The car slowed down and Tracy looked out the window to see the familiar campus buildings.

"Where is your castle, Cinderella?" Charlie asked.

"First moat on the right, your highness. Here I'll show you."

Tracy directed him up the drive toward her building. When the car stopped, she reached for Charlie's hand.

"I don't know how you did it, but you managed to turn the worst night of my life into something enjoyable."

"I forgot to tell you that in addition to Filene's and the empress gig, I sometimes moonlight as a fairy godmother."

Tracy leaned over, hugged him, and gave him a peck on the cheek.

"This time I really do believe you."

"You know, my fairy intuition (or it could be my old Irish soul) is telling me that this is all gonna turn out okay. It might get worse before it gets better, but I just have a feeling about you and this writer." He wagged his finger at her. "Oh, and by the way, I'm never wrong."

Tracy smiled sadly at him.

"Oh, and by the way, thank you Charlie. Good night."

#

That week Tracy purposely arrived to her seminar class right on the hour instead of her usual five minutes early. She saw Robin sitting in her regular seat across the room, the desk next to her empty. Instead of walking over there, she took a seat near the back door as far away as possible. Professor Coolidge looked up from her desk and immediately noticed the change. She stared directly at Tracy, her eyes narrowed, questioning. Tracy looked down at her notebook. Robin looked straight ahead.

When the class ended and people rose out of their seats, Professor Coolidge called out over the din, "Tracy, a moment please," and motioned for her to come up front.

Tracy walked over and stood to the side of the professor's desk.

"Have a seat," she said and smiled.

Professor Coolidge looked at her, a soft expression on her face, her arms folded against her middle.

"Anything you'd like to talk about?"

Tracy shook her head and looked down.

"Well, it's been hard not to notice the chill in the air between you and Robin lately and now this dramatic seating change. I'm just wondering if you're okay."

"Professor," she said, "I appreciate all you've done for me but with all due respect…"

"It's none of my business."

"No, I would never talk to you like that," Tracy assured her. "It's just." She hesitated and looked down again. "I can't. Not now, with finals and getting ready to go home. It's about all I can do to keep it together."

Professor Coolidge leaned toward Tracy. "And you don't think talking would help?"

"Right now it's hard to see if anything would help." Tracy looked up. "If it's okay with you, I'd like to leave it at that?"

"Yes, of course. But, Tracy, if you change your mind, please call me. I know I must seem impossibly ancient to you, but there have been times in my life when I've also wanted to sit as far away as possible from someone."

She wrote something down on a piece of paper, tore it off the pad and gave it to Tracy.

"This is my home number. Any time of the day or night would be fine if you want to talk. Really."

Tracy took the paper, and looked sheepishly at the professor.

"Thank you, that's very generous of you, especially in light of my past behavior."

"That's exactly how I see it, in the past. Take care, Tracy, and good luck with your finals."

CHAPTER FIFTEEN

After her last writing workshop at the BAYS drop-in center, Robin boarded the Red Line at Park Street in downtown Boston to head back to campus. She opened her American history textbook to study for the final she would be taking the next day, worried that she wasn't really prepared. The end of this semester had been so different from the last one when she'd felt on top of everything; her writing had come easily, and she'd breezed through her history term paper and finals. This semester had turned into a colossal struggle. Her writing was subpar, she was squeaking by in the psych seminar, and was hopelessly behind in her other two courses.

Everything had just gone horribly downhill since that night in New York. The only saving grace had been the group of kids at BAYS. Six of them came regularly to her writing workshop and a few others drifted in and out. She read them some of her stories, gave them a prompt ("write about a time that someone screwed you over" or "write about a time you had to steal from someone") and they were off and running. Their work was raw, passionate, and some of it was very good. It had been the only redeeming part of her pathetic life.

After the night with Murph, Tracy stopped speaking to her and avoided running into her. She'd even sat on the opposite side of the room in the seminar. Robin could see the worry on Professor Coolidge's face and wondered what Tracy had told her.

Really, she thought, what was there to tell after all? They'd each hurt the other one and now they had nothing. She remembered back to the last night she spent in the Village before starting Adams. How the life ahead of her had seemed like a great unknown. Now that she was going back to

New York for the summer, she was once again unsure of what her life would be like. She had her friends in the city, especially TJ and Sophia. But she'd lost something she once had—a kind of confident indifference that fueled her pursuit of casual sex with lots of different girls. *What am I going to do for all those months?* she wondered.

Two weeks later she was home lying in bed staring up at the ceiling in her room. She couldn't believe that she had once painted the ceiling in a black and white checkerboard pattern. Now it was making her nauseous and she had to close her eyes to avoid running to the bathroom. Her entire bedroom seemed juvenile, with posters of Joan Jett and Nirvana and the jacket covers from Joe Donovan's books tacked onto the wall. The only thing she still liked was her print of Robert Mapplethorpe's black and white self-portrait, the one in that book her mother had packed hidden in her jacket. She gazed at the close-up head shot of the artist dressed in a leather jacket, his tousled dark hair framing intense eyes, broad nose, and soft, thin lips. Robin had always wanted to emulate that image. It embodied all she imagined when she thought of a real artist.

Tomorrow she would start her summer job working for the ferry service. She managed to get the company to assign her to the line that carried visitors to Cherry Grove on Fire Island. This way, at least she'd be selling tickets to the mostly lesbian summer residents and day travelers who populated that sliver of a community so small, that it took only five minutes to walk across it. She'd also be working the concession stand next to the ferry dock.

It was your typical shitty seasonal job that she had stumbled on at the last minute, when some other kid they'd hired left suddenly after he was offered a part in summer stock. She'd have to work a few nights a week, but there would still be time to go into the city, and on slow days, she could get some writing done.

142

Even though the job had come through for her, nothing about this summer felt good. She had tried so hard to follow TJ's advice and toughen up. But instead she felt weak and lost, like a person who is going through the motions of living. Her heart just wasn't in it. That was the problem, her heart. She hadn't touched the Tracy journal since spring break. It lay hidden away in a drawer like damning evidence you want to make sure never sees the light of day.

When had these feelings about Tracy first surfaced? She thought back over the school year and realized there had always been an attraction, even on that day at the hall meeting. TJ had been right about the princess thing. Tracy hit Robin right where she was weakest. She was the beautiful girl with the mega-brain and that touch of vulnerability that made you want to slay dragons for her.

She recalled the vision of Tracy bent over a desk last December, frustrated by that Jane Austen paper, and how the two of them sat up late talking about *Emma* and *Pride and Prejudice* until they fell back exhausted onto the separate beds in Robin's dorm room. It was the first time that they had really connected, the first time she was able to see past the beautiful blonde hair and the accent and instead take notice of that vulnerability and, at the same time, Tracy's searing intelligence. Something inside Robin shifted that night and afterward everything changed. The next day she walked to the stationery store in the shopping center near campus and bought a new notebook to begin the Tracy journal.

My God, she thought, *I've been in love with her since last December and I'm just realizing it now?*

As she fought unsuccessfully to hold the tears back, all she could think was just how hopeless this situation was and how it made no sense. Hadn't Tracy flat out rejected her after that kiss on the dance floor? But then why did the Murph thing anger her to the point where she completely cut Robin off without even a goodbye at the end of the semester? That was perhaps the most hurtful thing of all. Before Robin could get to her, Tracy had just vanished.

"She wouldn't even say goodbye to me?" Robin asked Angie.

"She's wounded, Robin. She's angry and upset and I think she just wanted to run away."

"But why? *She* rejected *me*, Angie?"

"You're trying to make this into something rational when it's not. It's emotional. Tracy isn't thinking, she's just reacting."

"Well I'll agree with you there. She's not making any sense."

Angie nodded. "Maybe give it a few weeks and call her."

Robin shook her head. "And get hung up on or worse? No way. I'm not putting myself out there for her again."

Angie had stepped forward to hug Robin and then whispered into her ear.

"Just think about it."

#

As the summer weeks dragged on, Robin felt more and more adrift. Even her time with TJ was less fun than it used to be. Her friend tried to tempt her with a variety of girls who frequented the pier, The Well, and even the streets of the West Village, but Robin just hunched up her shoulders, shook her head, and kept walking.

One night at the bar, she was approached by a really cute woman with dark, curly hair cut above her shoulders; smoldering, chocolate eyes; and full lips. She was just about Robin's height and her tight jeans and midriff tank top showed off her very appealing curves.

"Hi," she breathed into Robin's ear, "I'm Amy. I've been watching you all night. Will you dance with me?"

Robin introduced herself and, instead of moving to the dance floor, they spent an hour or so talking. At one point, Robin spied TJ out of the corner of her eye flashing a victory sign with two fingers and then clapping her hands together. She gave her friend a weak smile. If she was ever going to get back in the swing of things, this was the girl who could help her do it.

A student at NYU majoring in American literature and women's studies, Amy had a summer job at Morrison Publishing, a company owned by Elizabeth Morrison, a high profile but closeted lesbian whose love life was a badly kept secret. Robin knew from just this little bit of information that Amy was someone she could talk to for hours. And she was clearly attracted to Robin. But yet, she couldn't get past conversation. When Amy leaned in to kiss her after they finally danced, Robin turned her head and saw the disappointment in those gorgeous brown eyes.

"I'm sorry," she said, looking down at the floor. "I'm very screwed up right now. Believe me, you're probably better off."

"Someone else beat me to you, didn't she?"

Robin swallowed hard and nodded.

Amy took her hand and asked, "Did she break your heart?"

Robin shrugged and walked away.

A few minutes later as Robin was leaving, Amy came up to her and handed her something.

"Here's my number. Call me when you get over her." She said this kindly and without rancor.

But it didn't matter how she said it. Robin was fuming. Amy had no right to presume that she could ever get over Tracy.

#

The next day Robin stood sulking against the wall of the pottery studio. Her mother looked up from the vase taking shape on her wheel.

145

"Robbie, those shorts are too loose. You're losing weight because you're not eating. Everything is hanging off you."

"Hmph," Robin responded and looked down.

"Honey, come here and sit with me."

Robin pulled a chair over and sat next to her mother. She looked at the vase on the wheel and marveled at her mom's ability to create art from wet clay. The shelves in the studio were filled with bowls, plates, and large platters in various stages of completion, some just dried brown clay and others with a layer of glaze waiting for those final touches that her mother added before she sold them.

Wendy Greene had become a successful artist. Her pottery sold well in a variety of stores and craft shows and she was often commissioned to create large pieces for weddings and anniversaries. Robin wondered if she could ever be that successful with her writing. It wasn't looking all that likely these days since she'd hardly written a thing in months.

"Robbie, you're miserable," Wendy said with great concern and sympathy. "You drag yourself through each day like you're moving through molasses. You eat practically nothing, I don't see you writing very much, and on more than a couple of occasions I've noticed your eyes are red from crying." She wiped her wet hands on a rag, rotated on her stool and clasped both of Robin's hands. "Will you talk to me?"

Robin looked down at the floor and moved a piece of hardened clay around with her foot.

"There's nothing to talk about. There's nothing I can do about it."

"Your heart's broken, isn't it, sweetie?"

Robin continued to look at the floor.

"What happened?"

Slowly Robin looked up at her mother, the one person she trusted more than anyone. She saw her compassion, her tenderness, and the unwavering love in her eyes. For probably the hundredth time that summer, tears welled up and the words poured out of her.

"Mom, she hates me. She rejected me and then she was angry that I was with someone else and she completely cut me off. God, she feels so far away from me, like we could never get back to one another."

Robin began crying in earnest. Big tears slid down her cheeks and she sniffed loudly. Her mother pulled her into a hug and let her cry.

"You're talking about Tracy, right?"

Robin nodded into her mother's wet shirt. "How did you know?" she said with a sniffle.

Wendy smiled sadly. "I paid close attention at our seder. I'd never seen you so happy to be with anyone. You were so alive."

"Oh, Mom, it couldn't be more different now and more horrible."

Wendy put her hands on Robin's shoulders and pulled back to look into her daughter's red eyes. "You fell in love with her, didn't you?"

Robin began to sob as she nodded her head.

"Robbie, honey, this is the hardest one. Your first love." She pulled Robin back into a hug. "How did the two of you leave things at the end of the semester?"

"We didn't," Robin said, still crying. "She left without even a goodbye. Angie said she's wounded and irrational."

"Hmm," Wendy said nodding. "Well, that could be a good thing actually."

Robin looked up at her mother and wiped her eyes with her arm. "How do you figure that?"

"The fact that she's emotional means she still cares."

"Even if that emotion is rage?"

Wendy gave a short laugh. "Especially. Why don't you try calling her?"

147

"I can't mom. Angie's also been after me about that, but I feel too scared that she'll just shoot me down again. I think if she really feels anything the next move is going to have to come from her."

"I'm not so sure about that, Robbie, but I do understand why you feel that way." Wendy leaned back a little. "Who was this other person that you flaunted in front of Tracy?"

Robin stared at her mother, clearly annoyed.

"I didn't flaunt anything! Tracy had already made it very clear to me that she wasn't feeling the same way I was." She softened a bit and looked down embarrassed. "Well, maybe there was a little bit of flaunting, but I was mostly trying to convince myself that, you know, I could move on, that I didn't need Tracy. But this thing with the other person turned out to be a major disaster."

Robin grabbed a piece of soft clay from the table next to Wendy's wheel and started to roll it around in her hands like Play-Doh, fashioning it into a long snake and then winding it around itself into a circle.

Wendy looked down at her daughter's hands and smiled. "You always used to make those when you were little." She picked up another piece of clay and rolled it into a small ball. "Why was this thing a disaster?"

"Oh Mom, I'm so embarrassed about it. I promised myself this was something I would never do with anyone, and then I did it." She lowered her voice to a whisper. "I faked it." She paused and looked up at her mother. "You know what I mean?"

"You faked an orgasm?"

"Mom!" Robin flattened the round clay snake into a pancake. "You just had to say yes, you knew. You didn't have to, like, be so explicit."

Her mother smiled.

"So you can run around the house talking about fucking and I can't even say the word 'orgasm'?"

148

Robin rolled her eyes and then looked at her mother seriously.

"Did you ever…you know?"

"Fake it? Of course." Wendy nodded her head. "It's almost a rite of passage. Well at least for a straight woman. I can't speak for lesbians. But for the record, never with your father."

Robin clasped her hands over her ears, a look of terror on her face.

"That is so much more information than I want or need. Now I have to spend the whole day getting that image out of my head."

Her mother laughed and a moment later, Robin lowered her hands and laughed with her.

With a sigh of relief, Wendy stood up from her stool and looked down at Robin.

"How about you try some spaghetti and meatballs? I have leftovers in the fridge that I can heat up for you."

"I'm not really hungry, but I'll try. Maybe one meatball."

Wendy pulled Robin up by her hands and once again looked at her lovingly, with a small smile on her face.

"Robbie, thank you for trusting me with this. I love you. You're an incredible young woman with a great life ahead of you."

She opened the door that led right into the kitchen and waited for Robin to go through first.

"I promise you, honey, it won't always feel as bad as it does today."

As she walked into the kitchen ahead of her mother, she stopped and turned back to her.

"I'm not so sure about that, Mom. But it did feel a little better to talk to you about it."

CHAPTER SIXTEEN

The Rocky Road ice cream barrel was nearly empty and Tracy had to reach way down inside to get a scoop for the cone that a customer had ordered. Her arm strained and she was on her toes to reach to the front of the freezer chest. After a day of this, her right arm ached all night, so she tried to work with her left one but it just wasn't as strong or coordinated.

Her mother had gotten her this job at The Biggest Scoop even though she had wanted to get something in a bookstore or a dance studio; even a movie theater would have been preferable. But the store was owned by the husband of one of the women in Luanne's garden club, so Tracy's mother was able to use her connections.

As part of her graduation present last summer her parents had excused her from having to work. This summer they told her she needed to earn her spending money for the school year. The job was torture. Either she was fighting with frozen solid ice cream or she was dealing with a crying child whose scoop of strawberry had fallen off the cone, the parents somehow blaming Tracy. The worst of it though was all the guys who hung out there and tried to hit on her. After spending a year up north, mostly in the company of other lesbians, it was jarring to once again be among straight men, especially southern straight men, who wielded their charm in a shockingly aggressive manner.

"Hey sweet thing," a high school-age boy had said to her as he paid for his chocolate shake, "you look like you could benefit from a nice romantic night under the moonlight. What do you say we meet up later? When do you get off?"

Tracy's standard response was to smile and shake her head no. At least once a week someone was so insistent that she had to call Brett or Jeff or even her father to come meet her at work when her shift was ending so the guy would back off.

At night she sat comatose at home, exhausted and depressed. She saw Brett and Jeff every few weeks and they did their best to entertain her at the movies or at the nearby lake. They also attempted to get her out to the bars, but she had no interest. Even the prospect of dancing provided little motivation.

Brett tried to joke around with her, making lascivious comments about women on the street.

"Now what about her, Tracy?" he asked, pointing to a well-dressed professional looking woman, a briefcase in her hand. "I bet she could rock your world in bed."

"I bet not," was all Tracy would respond, with sadness in her voice.

Jeff just stared at her as if he was trying to figure her out. She always felt like he could read her, almost better than anyone else, but he never offered a lot of opinions; only now and then would he utter a declaration.

"You're heartbroken," he said one day as they walked out of the ice cream shop after she'd called him for a rescue pick-up.

"I'm just exhausted from this awful job, Jeffy."

"Hmm," was all he'd responded.

Things at home with her parents were no better. She spent hours in her room avoiding her mother, and her father acted just like Jeff, watching her intently and not saying a word, until one morning when he did.

"Tracy, I have a colleague at Duke, Doctor Gloria Peters. Why don't we see if you can book some time with her?" her father said as Tracy moved uneaten scrambled eggs around her plate.

"I don't need a shrink, Daddy." She blew on her hot black coffee and took a sip.

"Well, let's look at all the evidence, shall we? You're in bed 'til late in the morning right up until you have to run out to work. You eat next to nothing. You come home and stay upstairs, going out only occasionally. You don't date…"

"Oh, so not dating is a sign of mental illness now?"

"You know that's not what I'm saying, darlin'," he said putting down his coffee cup. "You're showing most of the signs of depression and I think you could benefit from some help, and possibly, if it's called for, medication."

"Daddy, you saw my grades—two As, an A minus, and a D plus. Does that sound like someone who's depressed?"

"Well, it doesn't rule it out and your behavior this summer concerns me greatly."

"Well luckily there is an end point to this summer and I'll be out of your hair in a month or so. And I'll also be done with this horrible job Momma got me."

"Tracy, all summer jobs are horrible. You could be lifting heavy trays of food in some sweaty restaurant. You could be taking six-year-old children to the bathroom all day at a camp."

"I could have worked in a bookstore or a women's clothing shop, not in an ice cream-filled insane asylum. It's no wonder you think I need psychiatric help."

"If I thought it was just the job that was doing this to you," he said, "I'd tell you to quit in a heartbeat, but I worry that if you quit this job, you'll just spend those hours moping around the house in your pajamas all day, and then I'd really want to get you over to Doctor Peters."

Tracy stood up from the table, coffee cup in hand.

"Daddy, I'm fine," she said and walked out of the kitchen.

But she knew she wasn't. It was mid-July and she was feeling farther down in the dumps every day. She thought about Robin constantly, wondering what she was doing and who she was with. She missed her desperately. She talked to Angie on the phone a few times a week, and Angie confided that Robin was miserable as well.

"Is she seeing anybody or, you know, sleeping with anybody?" Tracy asked, not sure if she wanted to hear the answer.

"I doubt it. I'm not even sure how much she's writing. When I ask her, she changes the subject."

Tracy sat on the side of her bed, the phone cradled in her hand.

"She's not writing?" she said with alarm in her voice.

She was surprised and truly worried. Robin never stopped writing. Tracy began to pace the room.

"You're both sinking," Angie said, "but neither one of you will throw the other a life preserver. Why don't you call her?"

"I don't know. I just have no idea how she'll respond. Remember the last thing she said to me at school? 'That's fucked up, even for you.'"

"Well that was after you told her to watch out that she didn't catch VD from Murph."

"I know, but to say 'even for you' like I'm some kind of monster?"

"Tracy," Angie said clearly annoyed, "she was upset. Upset people say horrible things."

"Well that's what I'm worried about, that she's still upset."

She sat back down on the bed. "Look, I'll think about it. I know there's a possibility that it could turn out well, but I'm afraid that there's also the possibility that it could send me spiraling down even further. My daddy's after me to see a shrink because he thinks I'm depressed, and I just don't want to give him any more ammunition."

#

153

"Charlie? It's me Tracy. Remember from the bar? You drove me back to Adams?"

Tracy hoped that a talk with Charlie could work the same magic it had the night she walked down to Central Square after the awful scene with Robin and Murph.

"Cinderella!" he said in a cheerful voice. "Do you really think your fairy godmother would forget about you? How are you, my little girly girl? Still refusing to give up reading *Vogue*?"

Tracy giggled at the memory of their first conversation and then her tone changed.

"I'm kind of miserable, Your Highness. I was hoping you could wave your magic fairy godmother wand and make it all go away."

"I'd be more effective if I could just hand you a couple of Cosmos, but you're down there in the land of Dixie and I'm here living among rabid Red Sox fans. What's going on with your writer?"

Tracy sighed. "I wish she was my writer."

"Not yet, huh? Well I did say it would get worse before it got better, and I guess I was right."

"So far. When does the better part start?" Tracy wound the coiled yellow phone cord around her fingers.

"Oh Cinderella, I'm so sorry but my fairy godmother date and time functions are in the shop for repairs. You're just gonna have to figure that out on your own."

Tracy sighed and changed the subject.

"How's the Imperial Court?"

"On a little bit of a summer hiatus, although we did have an event in Ptown last weekend. Have you ever been?"

"Yes, once for a day with my friend Angie who grew up in the Boston area. She lives in Medford."

154

"Does she call it Meffa and leave out the d's?"

Tracy giggled, thinking of Angie's funny accent. "Yes, she does, though I think she's trying to speak more like a Kennedy. She wants to be a politician."

"People actually say that, that they want to be a politician? I thought they just make a pact with the devil and, poof, they get elected and start screwing us over."

"I think Angie will be different. She has a lot of integrity."

Charlie sighed. "They'll beat it out of her, I'm afraid. So other than the writer, how's your summer going?"

Tracy continued pacing and held the phone to her ear.

"There *is* nothing but the writer, Charlie. I have a shit job in an ice cream shop, boys there are hitting on me every day, I hardly ever go out, and I've almost stopped eating."

"Not even ice cream?"

"Especially not ice cream! This job has made me swear off it for good. What about you, still living like a nun?"

"That would be about right. I've often fantasized about moving to San Francisco and joining the Sisters of Perpetual Indulgence. Do you know them?"

Tracy laughed. "The Sisters of Perpetual Indulgence? Are they part of the Imperial Court?"

"No but they very well could be. They're a group of gay guys who dress up in nun drag but with heavy make-up and other outrageous accoutrements. They do street theater and protests. They have quite a following."

"Sounds like your kind of people. You could start a chapter in Boston?"

"Nah. I've got my hands full with the Court. When I think of the line-up of events for the fall, I just want to lie down on my fainting couch and sip a tall, cold Cosmo."

"Only if you make another one for me, okay?"

"Oh darling, you have succumbed to my drug of choice. I apologize for corrupting your pretty little blonde head."

"I was corrupted long before I met you, Charlie."

"Oh yeah? What's the most corrupt thing you've done in your young life?"

Tracy stopped pacing. "Hmm, let's see. So many to choose from. How does sleeping with my mother's best friend, a forty-something-year-old married woman, sound?"

Charlie coughed into the phone. His voice came out in a squeak.

"You're kidding, right?"

"Nope."

"Well then have another Cosmo, sweetheart. I no longer have any qualms about corrupting you."

They spoke for another few minutes and Charlie ended the conversation by once again repeating his prediction that "all will be well with you and that writer." Tracy started to wonder if there was any way he could be right.

#

It was a half-hour until her shift ended at seven o'clock when Tracy dialed the phone in the back office and reached Jeff.

"Jeffy, hey, it's me. Do you think you could come by the shop and get me at seven?" She paused. "No, not today. There is one creep but I can handle him. I just want to talk to you about something. How 'bout I buy us dinner?"

Thirty minutes later, Jeff Jordan strode through the pink front door of The Biggest Scoop looking around for Tracy. She saw him and reached over the counter to give him a hug.

"Hey, let me get these disgusting clothes off and we'll get going, okay?"

Tracy headed to the bathroom to get out of the neon pink polo shirt with the ice cream cone logo and The Biggest Scoop stitched into the fabric above her left breast. She put on a light blue tank top and her navy blue shorts, swapping them for the white jeans they made her wear. Her sandals felt good after a day spent in gym shoes. She put her work clothes and shoes in a bag, thinking it was probably time to throw them into the wash.

Jeff pulled his Honda Civic out of a parking space and headed in the direction of Chapel Hill.

"How's Luck Gourmet sound?" he asked Tracy.

"Good. I can have wonton soup there. I'm not eating a whole lot lately, but I think I can manage that."

Jeff nodded and was quiet.

It was an unspoken agreement between them that they head to Chapel Hill and not eat in Durham. While things were a lot better these days than in the past, it was still not too common for a white woman and a black man to be seen out together. Jeff was careful to avoid any kind of trouble, and Tracy felt protective of him.

Brett was interning for a Durham city councilor this summer and working on his campaign many nights. Jeff complained to Tracy that they hardly saw each other and, later in August, when he reported for football practice, they would both be impossibly busy. Tracy had only seen Brett a few times as well.

She and Jeff sat down in a red booth at the back of Luck Gourmet and ordered dinner.

"So what are we talking about tonight?" he asked, fiddling with his chopsticks.

"I want to know why you thought I seemed heartbroken the last time you came to get me from work?"

Jeff leaned forward toward Tracy and put his arms out in front of him. His Duke Blue Devils Football t-shirt fit snugly across his broad chest and shoulders. He'd cut his cornrows off and now wore his hair natural and extra short, so that when he started football again he could minimize the effects of the heat. He began to speak slowly and in a quiet voice.

"I told you over Christmas that I thought you were changing and that you were impatient about something. I didn't mention that I had a feeling there was someone who was preoccupying your thoughts and that you were waiting for something to happen with this person. I don't know how I knew that at the time, but it just made sense. You seemed less carefree, less focused on your conquests like when we were in high school. I figured there had to be someone who was filling up that space in you."

Tracy looked down at the table and played with a packet of sugar, shaking her head in amazement.

"It's like you can see right into my mind, Jeffy."

"You know me, Tracy," he said. "I watch closely and say very little until I'm asked, like now. It seems as if things have been difficult with this person since Christmas. Who is it?" he asked, "if you don't mind telling me."

In a small voice, Tracy replied, "Robin, from school."

"You've mentioned her a few times. What happened?"

"I don't really know," she said, looking up and facing him. "Things were good, though we were just friends and nothing more. But we were getting closer and there was definitely something happening between us."

Tracy paused, picked up her knife and began stirring her tea with it, watching the small swirls she was making as she continued the story. "Then when I went to New York at spring break, we were out dancing and she kissed me, I mean really kissed me. I kissed her back and then I suddenly pulled away and she ran from me and freaked out. After that she kept her distance. I said I was sorry…"

"Sorry for what?"

Tracy looked up at him. "For hurting her."

Their food came and they were quiet while the waiter set things down on the table. Tracy began to blow on the soup in her spoon.

"Were you sorry you pulled away?"

She put the spoon in her mouth and swallowed. Then she looked up at Jeff.

"I am now. But back then, I think I was scared. It was so intense with her. I had never experienced anything like that, ever. I've kissed lots of women but this was so different that it might as well have been called something else. I felt like I'd be going somewhere that I could never come back from. Does that sound crazy?"

"No, it sounds fearful," he said.

Jeff lifted strands of lo mein noodles with his chopsticks and held them up.

"How did you feel after spring break?"

Tracy began to cut the wontons in her bowl with the side of her spoon.

"I shut down and focused on school work. I did nothing but study and do research and then this other thing happened."

She put down her spoon and moved the bowl a little away from her. Jeff sucked an errant strand of noodle into his mouth.

"There was this person named Murph, the most annoying, boorish, and disgusting human being. She's a friend of Angie's girlfriend and was visiting from New York. Robin hooked up with her."

Jeff nodded for her to continue.

Tracy's tone was now indignant. "This happened right in front of me, Jeffy. They sat on the bed in Angie's room making out. I mean, right in front of me! With her hands all over Robin. I couldn't believe she would do that to me. That she would cheat on me that way. I was so upset I left and walked three miles—"

Jeff cut her off. "Tracy, Tracy, can you wind the tape back a minute? What did you just say?" His tone was insistent.

Tracy looked confused. "What? That I walked three miles? That they were kissing?"

"No," he said, shaking his head from side to side and leaning forward as far as he could. "That she was cheating on you."

"I said that?"

He nodded.

"Well, what I meant—"

Again, he interrupted. "No, you used that word for a reason."

He paused and his tone was now softer. He put his hand over hers. "It felt like that, didn't it? That she was cheating on you?"

"I...I guess so."

Tracy buried her face in her hands, and sat quietly like that for a few minutes shaking her head. Finally, she let out an anguished groan.

"Oh my God, Jeffy. I get it now. It's like I've spent the last semester living in two worlds at the same time. In one, Robin and I were friends who'd had a misunderstanding, but in the other one, we were together, like girlfriends, and the fact that I pulled away from the kiss didn't matter. In that reality I never stopped being with her. So, of course, when

160

she did this thing with Murph, it felt like she was cheating on me. That's why I was so angry."

She leaned back against the vinyl booth and shook her head again.

"Poor Robin," she said in an anguished tone, "I must have confused the hell out of her."

Jeff put his chopsticks down and nodded.

"So what now?" he asked.

"I don't know. I've screwed things up so badly, that I don't know how to fix them."

"You could start by telling her just what you told me."

Tracy picked up her small, round cup and took a gulp of tea.

"What if it's too late? What if she won't listen to me?"

"Then you'll know where you stand. Isn't knowing better than not knowing?"

Tracy thought quickly of Charlie and his prediction that things would turn out okay.

She took a deep breath. "Let me sit with it. You've given me a lot to mull over."

The waiter came by and cleared the table. Tracy had barely touched her soup.

"Jeffy, there's one more thing I want to bring up with you. It's not about me, it's about you."

"Me? What is it?"

"I think you should change your major to pre-med and become a psychiatrist."

"What?"

They were interrupted again by the waiter who brought them a small plate of pineapple cubes speared with toothpicks, two fortune cookies wrapped in clear plastic, and their check. Tracy twirled a toothpick between two fingers and spun around a piece of pineapple.

"Jeffy, I'm sure you'd make a fine engineer and you'd build all kinds of things, but you have a gift. You see things in people. You know how to help people."

"Tracy, I know *you* very well; you can't generalize and apply that to all people."

Tracy picked up a teaspoon and gestured with it toward Jeff.

"Jeffy, have you ever heard of Doctor Alan Rockwell?"

Jeff looked straight at her. "Well, you know Doctor Rockwell! He's a deacon in my church. A very important man."

"Well, he and his wife are friends of Momma and Daddy's. They've been over the house several times. Doctor Rockwell is the head of the North Carolina Black Psychiatrists Association and Daddy works with him to find talented African American students who want to become psychiatrists."

"I didn't know what kind of doctor he was. I just assumed he was, like, a cardiologist or something."

Jeff tore the plastic wrapping from his fortune cookie and cracked it open pulling out the strip of white paper inside. He read the short sentence and showed it to Tracy who read it aloud.

"Choose wisely at the fork in the road."

"Is that really a fortune or just advice?" he asked. "You know what Brett always says when he opens one of these and reads it?"

"Yes," she said with a smile. "He says, 'Help, I'm a prisoner in a Chinese fortune cookie factory.'"

"Yes, it's funny the first hundred times."

"Jeffy, I'd like to talk to Daddy about you and have you meet with him."

"Tracy, I don't know. I have a scholarship for engineering. I'd lose that."

"Doctor Rockwell has a million scholarships to replace it. That's not a problem. Besides, I know you already took biology and chemistry freshman year."

"Well only because I like science. Heck, *you* didn't want to go to med school and now you're encouraging me to go."

"That's because I don't like science. I only like psychology." She paused. "And intense Jewish writers from Long Island." She smiled sadly.

Jeff laughed quietly.

Tracy opened her fortune cookie and read it to Jeff.

"A prediction is about to come true." She held up the little strip and said, "Charlie."

"Who's Charlie?"

Tracy put the fortune in her purse and looked up at Jeff. "I'll tell you later."

"Tracy, I'm still not sure I have this gift you claim I have. But I'll agree to meet with your Daddy if it's that important to you."

"Jeffy, Daddy does this work with Doctor Rockwell because there's a horrible shortage of black psychiatrists in the South. They want to recruit and train people who'll be able to help folks in the community."

"Just because I'm black doesn't mean I can understand every other black person."

"True," she said, "but don't you think I could work with a lesbian patient more effectively than a straight psychologist could?"

Jeff shrugged his shoulders. "Possibly. I don't know. Look, I already agreed to the meeting."

Tracy brightened. "Great," she said standing, "let's get going."

She took her wallet out from her bag and grabbed the check from the table. After putting three dollars down for the waiter, she and Jeff walked to the register at the front. A few minutes later as they reached the car, Jeff opened the passenger door for Tracy.

"How 'bout we talk about something mundane on the way home, like movies?" he said as he sat down in the driver's seat. "I've about had enough of heavy topics for one day."

"Agreed," she said, buckling her seat belt. "But better than movies, how 'bout I tell you all about my fairy godmother. His name is Charlie."

Ah, the famous Charlie. Well, this oughta be good.

CHAPTER SEVENTEEN

Tracy paced the floor of her bedroom with the oval-shaped yellow phone cradled in her hand. Determined yet terrified she sat down on her bed and grabbed her old teddy bear, drawing him into a hug.

"Will you promise me that this will be okay, Rufus?" she asked, looking right into the bear's glassy black eyes. She laid him gently back down on the bed and sighed. "Non-committal as ever."

As she sat there, knowing what she had to do but afraid to do it, she remembered the day at the swap meet when she had come across the first edition of *Emma* by Jane Austen and had immediately decided not to tell the sellers about the treasure they had accidently acquired from the estate of Nanette Carlisle. She'd acted quickly thinking only of Robin and, looking back, it had been the right decision. Well, maybe it wasn't the most ethical decision, but from the standpoint of Robin and her, it had been right.

With new determination, she grabbed the phone, lifted the receiver and punched in the numbers she had committed to memory. As she heard the first ring, she breathed out and said, "okay here we go."

"Hello," Robin answered on the third ring.

"Hey, it's Tracy." She spoke softly right into the phone.

There were a few seconds of silence and then Robin spoke.

"Hi?" She drew out the word in a question.

Even with her heart pounding wildly in her chest and her whole body trembling, the sound of Robin's voice began to ease her misery.

"Robin," she said, "I need to say some things to you. Can you talk?"

"Yes?" Again, the same questioning tone.

Tracy took a deep breath and began, her words coming out in a torrent.

"I miss you. I miss you horribly. I miss us. I want things to be...no, I don't want things to be the way they were. I want things to change. I want to be with you. I want us to be together. I was crazy to pull away from you that night in New York. But I was scared and it's how I reacted in the moment. When you kissed me and then I kissed you, I had no idea what to do with that. I've never felt about anyone what I feel for you.

"I know, looking back now, that that was maddening. And I know it was horrible for you, that you took a risk and I rejected you. And then all I could say was I was sorry I hurt you, instead of I was sorry I did what I did. Oh God, if I could take it all back, it would be so different.

"Robin, I've never wanted anyone the way I want you. I'm miserable. I'm not eating, I mope around all the time, I keep thinking if I call you you're gonna hang up on me. I'm a complete and total mess over you. And all I want is you."

Tracy stopped to catch her breath. There was silence on the other end of the line.

"Wow," Robin said, breathing out the word as she exhaled. "I never thought I'd hear any of that from you. I mean I dreamed about it, I wished for it, but I never thought it would really happen. Especially not after what I did to you."

Tracy relaxed a little and sat cross-legged in the middle of her bed.

"I don't care about any of that. Well, that's not entirely true, I still do a little."

"Tracy, I miss you too. I'm a mess too. And I'm also sorry I hurt you."

"Angie said you're not writing. Is that true?"

"Yeah, it is. I seem not to be able to."

"Oh my God," Tracy said as she fully understood the toll this had taken on Robin.

166

"I'm not eating much either. The other day I had a meatball and my mother practically declared a national holiday."

Tracy smiled. This was Robin, her Robin.

"I know. Even my Momma, who has always obsessed about my weight, has been trying to tempt me with all kinds of food. She even went so far as to bake a pecan pie," she said. "And Daddy is threatening to send me to a shrink because he thinks I'm depressed."

There was another short pause and then Robin spoke.

"Did you mean what you said before, about wanting us to, you know, be together?"

"Every word," Tracy said. "What do you want?"

"You. I have for a long time."

Tracy's anxieties vanished and the knot in her stomach unraveled. She lay back on her bed greatly relieved, but there were still some things she needed to know.

"Did you hook up with Murph to get back at me?" she asked, trying not to sound angry.

"Not completely. I can't say that wasn't part of it, but the main reason was to prove to myself that I could move on, that I didn't need you. But, I have to tell you, this thing with Murph, it was a total disaster."

"It was? Why?"

"Because, Tracy, I faked it."

"What do you mean, you faked it?"

"You know, the orgasm. I faked it."

Tracy grinned, a loud cheer reverberated in her head.

"Did she notice?" she asked, trying not to laugh.

"No, of course not. She thought she was magnificent."

Tracy couldn't hold back any longer and she laughed. Robin laughed with her.

"Why did you, you know, fake it?"

"Because it wasn't happening naturally and I didn't want to be in bed with her forever. To tell you the truth, I'm kind of embarrassed about it. It's a shitty thing to do to anybody."

Tracy felt like she had to ask Robin every question she had about that night so she could finally put it to rest.

"Why don't you think it was happening? Was she that bad?"

"I think it's obvious why it wasn't happening. It's because she wasn't you. You're the only one who could have, well you know, succeeded. Look, last week I was in the city and some girl practically threw herself at me in the bar. She was pretty, smart, we had a lot of similar interests..."

"Robin, I don't think I want to hear..."

"Hold on, I'm telling you this because nothing happened! I wouldn't even let her kiss me. You know what she did before she left that night? She handed me her number and said, 'call me when you get over her.' It really pissed me off that she would presume that I could ever get over you."

Tracy was smiling. "Okay, I changed my mind. I did want to hear that story."

Robin chuckled and then continued, more serious now.

"Angie said you hate your job."

"Ugh, it's loathsome. Kids crying, boys hitting on me, ice cream that's frozen like a glacier."

"No girls hitting on you?"

"Who knows? But I don't want that either, unless you'd like to book the next flight down here and visit me there tomorrow." Her tone became flirty and light. "I'll give you any flavor you want, free of charge."

"Hmm, I think you just propositioned me."

"I did. I want you."

168

"Same here, but the flavor I want usually isn't found in a tub of ice cream."

As much as the conversation had become great fun, not to mention incredibly arousing, Tracy remembered that she had more to say to Robin. She sat up.

"I wanted to tell you a few more things, just to get everything out in the open."

"Not about ice cream flavors, I presume, right?"

"No, I'm fixin' to get serious again."

"You said 'fixin' just for my benefit, didn't you?"

"Robin, would you like to hear what I have to say or are we gonna have to re-fight the Civil War?"

Robin laughed. "So touchy, aren't we? Go ahead."

"Well, I had dinner with Jeffy the other night, you know who I'm talking about right?"

"Yes, Jeff, of Brett and Jeff."

"Right. And I decided to talk to him about you and what happened. I was telling him the Murph story…"

"Oh he must love me now."

"He's not like that. But anyway, I told him that I was angry with you because you had cheated on me."

"Huh? But I didn't. We weren't even…"

"Right," said Tracy. "He latched right on to that as well. And when he asked me about it, I didn't even realize I had said it, that I had used the word 'cheated.' And then, after we talked some more, it suddenly dawned on me. The reason it felt like you had cheated on me was because I'd been living two different realities in my head. In one we were just friends and in the other we were a couple. And even though I stopped kissing you in the

169

bar because I was so scared of what that would mean, at the same time, probably in the next second, we were more than friends." She paused.

"I think I'm following this," Robin said a bit uncertainly.

"I know. It's pretty screwed up, but it does really explain why I got so angry that I wouldn't sit next to you anymore in the seminar and why I left school without saying goodbye, both of which, by the way, I'm truly sorry for."

"Hold on. You know, this really does kind of make sense to me now. I was going crazy because you kept doing things, like taking my hand in the car before the seder or staring at me with all this intensity, and then nothing. We would always just go back to being the way we were. You even kissed me on the mouth when we were at BAYS doing our project."

"Yes," she said with a sigh, "all of that was part of it. I was with you and not with you, sometimes in the span of only a few minutes, and, of course, I was making you crazy over it. I just wasn't aware enough to know it myself. And because I was so terrified to come to terms with what I was feeling for you, I had a built-in reason to not want to figure it all out."

Tracy stood up and began to pace.

"Now that I've told you how insane I am, I hope it's not a deal breaker."

"Oh God, no!" said Robin. "It clears up so much. I could never figure out what you were doing and how you were feeling, but I think I get it now."

Relieved, Tracy sat back down on the bed.

"I have another story to tell you that's not quite so heavy. I think you'll like it."

"Okay, it seems to be the night for true confessions."

"Yes, I really do want everything out in the open now. I want us to start things off right."

"Me too. So go ahead. I'm in bed waiting for my bedtime story."

"You're in bed, huh?" Tracy couldn't help herself.

"Yes, are you?"

"Yes, we're both in bed." Tracy said lying back down.

"We're both in bed together."

"Don't I wish," said Tracy. She breathed out. "Okay, let me tell you this story."

"Wait, can I just tell you first how good it feels to hear your voice again?"

"Hmm, yours too. As soon as we started talking I felt like the cloud that had been hovering over me was lifting."

"Okay, story time," Robin said in the voice of an eager child.

Tracy chuckled. "You're sure now?"

"Yes, I'm in my pajamas."

"Oh that won't do."

"I didn't realize this was *that* kind of story."

"Well, yes and no. Okay, here it is. Remember last New Year's Eve I went to a party with Brett and Jeffy?"

"Yes and you had sex with some woman who I then murdered with my bare hands."

Tracy laughed. "I always wondered what became of her. Anyway, before I left the party with her, I put her through this test that I always gave potential, you know..."

"Sex partners?" said Robin.

"Well, yes. I'd decided at some point that a woman was only going to be good in bed if she could dance well. So I watched her and declared her to be adequate."

"There's a ringing endorsement."

171

"I was a bit desperate that night. Like I said, I couldn't admit that what I wanted was you and I had all this nervous energy. Jeffy said I seemed impatient, and so I decided what I needed was sex. Oh wait, there's another part to this I have to tell you before I go on."

"Let me know the next time you need help plotting out a novel."

"Let *me* know the next time you need help understanding Carl Jung."

"Touché," Robin said laughing. "So what's the other part?"

"Remember when we went to the bar in Boston with Angie and Nicky during finals last year?"

"Yeah?"

"Well, you didn't notice, but I watched you dance and I couldn't believe how good you were. I was getting turned on just from watching you and all I kept thinking was, 'she must be amazing in bed.' It got so I had to go outside to cool off."

Robin was laughing. "You're kidding?"

"No I am not. So back to New Year's Eve. I get to this woman's apartment and, well, let's just say her performance was turning out to be less than adequate."

"So much for the dancing test."

"No, I think I made a mistake and gave her dancing too much of the benefit of the doubt when I said it was adequate."

"You mean like grade inflation?"

"Something like that. Anyway, I lay back on her bed and I started to think about you dancing. But in this fantasy, I was the one dancing with you and it was incredibly hot. We were staring at each other and moving back and forth, back and forth."

Robin interjected. "Wow, it's getting kind of warm in here."

"Exactly, and I must say, that little fantasy did the trick. I came quickly and very hard. And just like you said about Murph, this woman thought she was magnificent."

Robin chuckled. "That's quite a story."

"I thought you might like it."

"Tracy," Robin began in a careful tone, "I have to ask this. Am I going to wake up tomorrow and all of this will still be true? You'll still want us to be together? You'll still want to sleep with me?"

"What time do you have to be at work tomorrow?"

"My shift starts at ten, why?"

"Call me when you wake up."

"Won't you be asleep?"

"I don't care. I want yours to be the first voice I hear when I wake up and the last one I hear when I go to sleep."

"Geez, I'm speechless."

"Are you glad I called?"

"Are you kidding?" Robin replied incredulous. "I feel like the earth started spinning again."

Tracy smiled. "That's because it did. Goodnight, sweetheart."

"Wow, sweetheart." Robin breathed out.

"Is it okay that I called you that?"

Robin's tone softened and she said in a whisper, "yes baby, it's very okay. I'll talk to you in the morning. Good night."

#

The next morning, Tracy placed the phone back on the receiver after finishing a short call with Robin. She sat up in bed smiling with Robin's voice echoing in her head. They made a plan to talk every night at nine and a little later on the nights when one of them had to work evenings.

173

Is this what it feels like to be in love, she wondered? She felt excited and giddy, like a walking cliché. This must be what all those love songs she listened to were talking about. She'd thought of telling Robin how she felt, but worried that because things were still so fragile and new she should wait. What if Robin wasn't in the same place? She hadn't used the word "love." Tracy had promised Robin openness and no secrets, so she knew that sooner or later she'd have to be honest about this. But maybe she could hold off until they were together at school.

Tracy put the phone back on her night table and stood up full of energy. She ran down the stairs and met her mother in the kitchen.

"Morning Momma," she said in a loud voice and kissed her mother on the cheek. "Could you make some of those cheese grits I like and scrambled eggs and bacon? I'm starving."

Luanne Patterson looked up from her newspaper and stared at Tracy.

"Who are you and what did you do with my daughter?" she asked. Then she smiled and walked over to the refrigerator.

At that moment, her father came into the kitchen dressed in khaki pants and a light blue shirt.

"Tracy, you're awake at an early hour."

"Mornin' Daddy. I asked Momma to cook me breakfast. Do you want to eat with me?"

He poured himself a cup of coffee and looked at his watch.

"I have a patient in a little while, so I've got to get going. But it's nice to know that you're eating again."

"Yes. So now I won't have to hear any more talk of Doctor Peters, right?"

"Sounds like you just may run out the clock on this one. Let's see how things go over the next few days."

Later that week, Tracy punched in Robin's number at nine o'clock. It was her turn to call.

The phone rang once and Robin picked up.

"Hi gorgeous, how was your day?"

"It just got a whole lot better."

"Mine too."

The sound of Robin's voice so happy and playful put Tracy in a similar mood.

"I thought about you all day. It's starting to make the ice cream melt."

Robin chuckled. "That's just you trying to get fired from that sucky job. They'll find you knee deep in a sea of mint chocolate chip and can your beautiful ass."

She thinks I have a beautiful ass. Tracy continued the flirty banter.

"Do you want to know what I was thinking about you today?"

"Will I have to turn up the air conditioner?"

"Hmm, possibly."

Tracy lay back on her bed getting comfortable. "I was thinking about the first time we'll see each other in a few weeks. And I was imagining what it will be like to feel your hands on me."

Robin responded in a low soft voice. "You mean when I touch your cheek and then lower my hand and brush it against your shoulder and down your arm?"

Tracy could hardly speak. All she managed was some accelerated breathing followed by, "Oh Robin."

Robin's voice was husky. "You know where I'd want to go next? I'd want to move my hand to feel your soft breasts and linger for a long time on first one nipple and then the other, getting more and more excited as they stiffened at my touch."

Tracy breathed out and groaned. Then she remembered what she had resolved to tell Robin and sat up.

"Robin, hold on. Believe me, this is having the intended effect; I'm laying here on my bed in a puddle. And I'm in no way pulling back, I promise. But I don't want our first time to be phone sex. I want it to be in person. I don't want to just hear you, I want to see and feel and taste you. I want all of it the first time. Do you get what I'm saying?"

Robin's tone was still playful and reassuring. "You know this waiting will involve a lot of cold showers over the next few weeks?"

Tracy smiled with relief. "You're not upset with me then, are you?"

"No. I'm just dying to be with you and I guess I thought this was better than nothing."

"I know. I want you so much too, and I'm not being a prude about the phone sex. If we'd already, you know, been together, I'd be the one initiating it. I just want everything with us to be special. I want to look in your eyes when I come and I want it to be because you touched me, not because I touched myself. Okay?"

Robin breathed out audibly. "I can't argue with that."

"I know after this, it's gonna be hard to switch gears, but will you tell me about your day?"

"Well, there's good news and not such good news. Which do you want first?"

"Let's start with the good news since I just had to deliver some bad news about the phone sex."

"Okay. I finished a story. The one I was telling you about with the homeless kid who hides out in a movie theater."

"Oh, Robin that's wonderful. You'll have something to turn in to Joe when you get back."

"Yes, by the skin of my teeth. Who knows, maybe there's a second one inside of me, especially now that my muse is back."

Tracy crossed her legs and drew them close.

"You mean me? I'm your muse?"

"You appear to be, sweetheart. I wasn't doing so well when things were bad between us and now I'm cruising along."

"But you were writing before you even knew me."

"Yes, but I did my best work freshman year, at least before spring break."

"Robin, I don't know what to say. I'm honored."

"Ah, but with great honor comes great responsibility. Being a muse isn't all it's cracked up to be, you know, not since they busted the muse union and sent most of the jobs overseas. Now the hours are long, there's a lot of pressure, and you can never quit."

"Still," Tracy said, "I accept this honor with all its limitations. I will forever be the official muse of Robin Greene, America's most celebrated writer. I will guide you all the way up the *New York Times* best seller list until you get to the National Book Awards."

Robin let out a short whistle. "Wow, talk about pressure. You're a very demanding muse."

"I work with a very talented writer and I expect great things from her." Tracy became more serious. "Now tell me the bad news."

"Well, I called Peter Delany from BAYS today. Remember him?"

"Of course. Why did you call him?"

"Just to check in, see how things were, and tell him that I wanted to start the writing group again in September."

"Oh Robin, that's great. I'd love to go back there with you."

"I'd like that too. A lot."

"Yes, and this time you won't have to wonder what's going on when I kiss you."

Robin ignored the comment and went on with her story.

"So Peter told me that the state had slashed some of their funding and they might have to cut back the program by helping fewer kids."

"Oh wow, that's horrible."

"I know. I wish I could do something. I wish I had money to give them. Too bad we don't know anyone who'd be able to help."

Tracy stood up from her bed and began to walk around her room.

"Wait, Robin, I do know someone. Remember Charlie, who I told you about the other night?"

"The empress fairy godmother?"

"Yes, his Imperial Court raises money for gay organizations. I bet they'd do some kind of an event for BAYS."

"Oh Tracy, that would be incredible. Can you call him?"

"Yes, I'll do it tomorrow. I'm sure they'll come through."

"See how much better my life is now that you're back in it?"

"See how you always get me to be the best person I can be?"

#

It was the weekend before the dorms opened for the beginning of school. Tracy had stopped counting the days and started counting the hours 'til she would see Robin. Today had been her last day of work at The Biggest Scoop and she was pacing across her bedroom floor waiting for the phone to ring at nine o'clock.

She grabbed the receiver immediately as soon as she heard the ring.

"Hi," she said, unable to keep the excitement out of her voice. "I can't wait to tell you what I did today."

"You finally torched the place, huh? Was that how you said goodbye?"

"No even better. This was inspired. You ready to hear?"

"Well, I was going to tell you how wonderful you are and how happy you make me but, nah, go ahead."

Tracy didn't skip a beat. "Okay, so this guy is bothering me, you know the usual stuff?"

"I don't know. This never happens to me."

"Consider yourself lucky. It's infuriating. But anyway, my shift is about to end and he says to me, 'so, when do you get off?' And do you know what I said?"

"I have a feeling it wasn't seven o'clock."

"Nooooo," Tracy replied. "He said, 'So, when do you get off?' and I said to him, 'when I'm in bed with my girlfriend.'" She paused. "Isn't that great?"

Robin dissolved into laughter. "You did? You actually said that? That's hysterical. That's something I would do." She couldn't stop laughing. "What did he say?"

"He stood there dumbfounded. So I just walked to the back, changed my clothes, and I was outta there for the very last time."

Tracy could hear Robin applauding.

"Bravo, bravo, a virtuoso performance by a lesbian in a leading role. I'm really proud of you. That took a lot of guts."

"Thank you, thank you. I want to thank the Academy and my girlfriend, Robin Greene, who was the inspiration for this brilliant comeback."

"Girlfriend, huh?"

"Right?" said Tracy.

Robin answered immediately and positively. "Oh, yes, right." And then more slowly, enunciating each word, "And you're my girlfriend, right?"

"Yes, and so happy to finally have the title."

179

"So how many hours is it?" Robin asked.

Tracy looked at her bedroom clock. The red digital numbers said nine forty-one. She did a quick calculation in her head. "One hundred and seventeen, if I'm getting the math right."

"Ugh, that sounds so much longer than five days."

"Yes, but when you wake up, sweetheart, it'll be down to about one hundred and six."

"I'd much prefer just six. Six hours. I could rent a few movies, take a long walk, and then it would be time."

CHAPTER EIGHTEEN

Robin drove back to school with her stuff crowded into the old Sentra that she'd bought with her parents' help. Their share had been her high school graduation present and she had used her bat mitzvah money to cover her share, with a remaining amount reserved for insurance. As a sophomore, she was allowed to have a car on campus and she looked forward to the freedom it would give her and, she thought hopefully, Tracy.

As she paid the toll on the Massachusetts Turnpike and headed toward campus, she realized that Tracy was already there. Her plane had landed at eleven-thirty that morning. They'd had a brief call very early before Tracy left for the airport.

"I'm a little nervous," Robin had confessed. "Are you?"

"No. I'm calm and happy and dying to see you. Don't be nervous and drive safely. We're finally down to single digits in the number of hours count."

"We're good then? You still want…"

"You. Only you. I've gotta get going. My mother's driving me crazy this morning."

The dorm lottery had been held right before spring break last semester and they had been able to get their first choice—a four-person suite in Meyerson, which had the nicest rooms as well as kitchens on every floor. The suite included its own full bath and four bedrooms. Barbara would be completing the foursome. Tracy had volunteered her room as the meeting place because it was a little larger than the other three. But now Robin hoped she'd be spending very little time in her own room, except maybe to write, so instead it could become a kind of living room space.

Maybe I'm getting a little ahead of myself, she wondered. *Would Tracy want them to sleep together every night?*

God, we haven't even done it once and I'm already thinking we're gonna be sharing the same bed all the time. What if I'm a dud in the sack and she's disappointed? We've never talked explicitly about sex and what we each like. How will I know what she wants?

Pulling up to the dorm building, Robin found a handcart that someone else had just finished using and piled her stuff onto it, leaving her stereo and computer in the car. She parked in the student lot making sure her new purple window sticker was visible and walked back to the dorm with the valuable items she had kept in the car. She retrieved the cart and took it up in the elevator to the third floor.

This new building was a huge step up from their freshman dorm. There was no cinderblock. The walls were plaster painted in vibrant primary colors. She felt renewed walking past the common rooms with their natural light; oak tables; sunny yellow couches; and arm chairs with thick, comfortable-looking cushions.

Once on the third floor, she wheeled the cart down to their suite and opened the bright blue main door, turning first to her room. She began throwing her things off the cart and onto the floor, only taking care to make sure that her stereo and computer were handled more carefully and placed on the bed. In her impatience, she tipped the cart and let the rest of her things fall over. She thought of just leaving it there, but there was probably some poor fool pulling up to the front who would need it as she had.

She ran down the hall with the empty cart and saw Grayson, a guy from her writing program, waiting for the elevator.

"Grayson!" She greeted him with a hug. "Hey man, let's catch up soon. Can you do me a favor and take this down to the front door? I need to meet someone."

With the cart out off her hands, she sprinted down the hall back to the suite door and then stood quietly catching her breath and getting ready for the big moment.

She knocked on Tracy's door and a familiar voice answered happily, "Come in."

As she walked in and closed the door behind her, she saw Tracy standing in the middle of the room, next to all of her unpacked suitcases and boxes. Dressed in light pink shorts and a button down, sleeveless, white blouse, her hair hanging loose over her shoulders, her physical beauty took Robin's breath away and she stood and stared for a minute. Tracy stared back smiling.

Robin glanced to the side and saw the bed all made with two pillows, yellow pinstripe sheets, and a white cotton blanket. She smiled and gestured with her head.

"I see you made the bed," was the first thing she said to Tracy.

"Wouldn't you agree that I have my priorities in order?" She paused and looked directly at Robin. "Hi," she said.

"Hi."

Tracy took a step toward her and spoke, her voice almost a whisper. "Come here. There'll be no more pulling away. Not ever."

She senses that I'm worried, thought Robin.

Robin closed the space between them and gently took Tracy's upper arms in her hands, pulling her close. They both moved their heads forward for the kiss and then there was nothing else but the two of them and their mouths coming together. This time Tracy's tongue found Robin's open mouth and while they kissed Robin explored Tracy's bare arms and then her shoulders, migrating around to her back. She moved her mouth to Tracy's neck and began to kiss the unbelievably soft skin there, listening to Tracy's quickening breathing and exclamations. Their legs became entwined and Robin began to move the lower part of her body against Tracy.

"Oh Robin, yes, yes. Please don't stop that."

Robin moved to Tracy's ear, lightly bit her soft earlobe and whispered, "Tracy, finally."

Tracy's mouth was now on Robin's neck and her hands in Robin's thick, wavy hair.

"I want you so much," Tracy whispered. "It's all I can think about. I'm so ready for you."

Robin felt her hands trembling as she held Tracy. She wanted this to be perfect.

Tracy moved her mouth back to Robin's and they began to kiss deeply again. Tracy began pulling Robin's t-shirt out of her shorts. She felt hands on her bare waist. The touch was intoxicating. Tracy pushed up the t-shirt clearly wanting it out of the way.

Robin broke the kiss and moved back to Tracy's ear.

"Tracy, baby," she said, her breathing heavy. "What do you like? I need to know what you want me to do."

Tracy's voice was strained with desire and need.

"Everything. Everything from you," she said.

Robin's intense desire helped her find her courage and she returned to Tracy's mouth, unbuttoning the white blouse and releasing the bra clasps quickly. She reached around to the front and removed both the blouse and the white lace bra while moving her tongue around Tracy's. Her first touch of Tracy's soft breasts sent them both reeling and swaying, and when Robin's fingers felt the already hard nipples, Tracy gasped.

184

"I don't think I can do this standing up," she whispered into Robin's ear.

Robin guided her to the bed and pulled her own t-shirt over her head, along with her bra. She lowered Tracy onto her back and looked down at her, again overcome by her beauty, especially now that her gorgeous breasts were visible and begging to be touched. Robin felt a throbbing between her own legs. She lay down on her side next to Tracy and unbuttoned the pink shorts, pulling them and the pink underwear underneath them down Tracy's strong, tanned legs. Tracy lifted her bottom to help.

Tracy pulled at the waistband of Robin's denim shorts.

"Off," was all she could manage to say.

Robin undid her shorts and pulled them off along with her underwear.

Tracy turned to face Robin and they looked at each other's naked bodies in wide-eyed wonder. Tracy's paler, thinner but curvy form, with blonde hair cascading below her shoulders onto her chest; Robin's slightly shorter, darker, stocky body, her shoulders broad and her wavy hair falling onto her forehead.

"Please," Tracy urged her, "take me now."

Robin moved on top and began kissing Tracy again. Her hands kneaded both breasts and then slid down to the nipples, which she rolled between two fingers. She lowered her head and kissed Tracy's neck and then her chest, all the while playing with her dark pink nipples.

Tracy's head was stretched back on the pillow and she was moaning and urging Robin on. Robin took one nipple in her mouth and Tracy let out a loud gasp and then a moan. With a free hand, Robin moved down the length of Tracy's stomach, landing on the soft patch of light brown hair between her legs.

Tracy moved her legs apart and Robin slid her hand down further until she felt the incredible wetness there. She moved her head back up to Tracy's ear and began to speak in a whisper as her fingers moved between the soft, wet folds.

"You are amazingly beautiful," she said as she touched the stiffened clit and then began to circle it. "I want this more than I've ever wanted anything." Her fingers slid inside Tracy, who responded with a loud, "ohhhhnn." Robin began to move in and out, listening to Tracy's labored breathing.

"I want you to come hard for me, baby. I want all of it."

As she continued moving her fingers, she touched Tracy's clit with her thumb and Tracy's back arched up.

"Now baby," Robin urged as she increased the pressure on Tracy's clit. "Now!"

Tracy screamed out "Robin!" and Robin felt the seismic movement from inside as Tracy's body bucked and rocked. She kept the movement going as another wave came over Tracy. When that wave slowed to a ripple, Robin's hand came to a rest. She pulled Tracy to her and held her in her arms. They were both quiet for a few minutes while Robin felt aftershocks course through Tracy's body. Her cheeks had a light pink glow and there was a slight smile on her face, her eyes still closed. Robin gazed at her in wonder. She had never looked more beautiful than she did in that moment.

Finally, Tracy lifted her head from Robin's chest.

"What did you do to me?" she asked, her voice full of amazement.

"Was it…good?" said Robin.

"Oh my God, 'good' isn't even close. We need to go to spectacular, stunning, unlike anything I've ever felt."

Robin tightened her grip on Tracy and kissed the top of her head. Relief and gratitude spread through her body and she relaxed.

Tracy began to kiss her softly and then her energy changed and she became more insistent, pushing her tongue into Robin's mouth and running her hands down Robin's chest on the way to her breasts.

"I'm only hoping I can be half as good for you," she said before taking Robin's nipple into her mouth and sucking it hungrily, her teeth nipping it gently.

Robin felt the sensation go right to the place between her legs. She really needed to come. Tracy was driving her wild with desire.

Tracy moved her hand to Robin's face and caressed her cheek and then slid a finger into Robin's mouth. Robin sucked and teased the finger with her tongue and Tracy moved it in and out of Robin's mouth. The vision of Tracy's tongue accidently licking Robin's fingers at the seder sprang to her mind.

Tracy lowered her hand and now both hands were on each side of Robin's torso, enabling her to slide her body down. She kissed Robin's belly and the mound of dark curly hair beneath it.

Robin took a deep breath when she saw where Tracy was heading. She had never allowed anyone to do this to her, although she had done it to lots of girls herself.

"Tracy," she said with some anguish in her voice. "I've never let…"

Tracy raised her head and looked into Robin's eyes with desire and understanding.

"Will you let me?" she asked.

Robin was quiet for a few seconds thinking it over and staring into Tracy's green eyes. If this was going to happen with anyone, then it would be with Tracy, the woman she loved.

"Okay," she said and nodded.

Tracy moved down between Robin's legs and gently kissed the inside of her thighs, migrating toward the center. Robin was aching with need and the sensation of Tracy's tongue in that throbbing place sent a jolt through her body. Tracy was gentle at first, licking her outer lips and then moving inward to Robin's clit. In an instant Robin knew she wanted this and she lowered her hands to Tracy's head, pushing it down to add pressure. While she caressed Tracy's soft blonde hair, she felt the sensation of her tongue as it flicked across her clit and she moaned, feeling her body start to climb to where she needed to go. Tracy began to suck gently and then Robin felt two fingers enter her, which made her shout out Tracy's name. Tracy kept her fingers inside, stroking the soft spot she found there and began to suck on Robin's clit. That was all that was needed. Robin's entire body shook, conscious thought left her and her world was centered between her legs. She held tight to Tracy's head and called out, "Oh God, Oh God, Oh God, Tracy!" as she rose to heights she had never experienced and then floated back down to earth.

Tracy quickly scooted her body back up to hold Robin who clung to her.

"Now I know what you meant when you said 'what did you do to me.'"

Tracy was quiet for another minute and then looked at Robin and smiled.

"So I was the first, wasn't I?" she asked in a self-satisfied tone.

Robin ran her hand down the side of Tracy's body.

"Let's not get all high and mighty and smug about it. I have an image as an urban lothario to protect, you know."

"Your lothario days are officially behind you, if you know what's good for you," Tracy said. "Right?"

"Right," Robin replied in a tone of mock reluctance. "But don't be telling that Angie Antonelli about this. I have her convinced that I'm vastly more experienced than she is."

Tracy traced the outside of Robin's mouth with her finger.

"Well maybe in all ways but one. I have a feeling that Angie's had a few more mouths between her legs than you, sweetie."

"Shhh," Robin said licking Tracy's finger and tasting herself on it. "If you let this be our little secret, I'll do what I did to you again."

"Hmmm, that's a bargain I can live with."

"I'm glad because you and I are very far from done, baby," said Robin as she lowered her mouth onto Tracy's nipple.

"Oh God, yes, that's for sure."

#

Over the next few days, they were in the bed more than they were out of it. Angie walked in on them at one point and was delighted to see that they'd finally "closed the deal," as she put it. Robin strode around the room naked, picking up and putting on the clothes that she had discarded on the floor while Tracy stayed in bed with the sheet pulled up to her neck.

"Tracy, I've seen you naked before," Angie said, shaking her head.

"Not in this situation you haven't," Tracy said, embarrassment creeping up her neck to her cheeks.

Robin chuckled.

"Angie, turn your back for a minute and let her put some clothes on."

Angie rolled her eyes and turned her back.

On the first day of classes, Tracy and Robin stayed in bed all morning since neither of them had a class until the afternoon. Robin was holding Tracy from behind and kissing her neck when the phone rang.

There was one line for the whole suite, so the call could be for any of them. Robin rose out of bed with a groan and picked up the phone. It was her mother.

"Hi, honey, I'm just calling to check in," Wendy Greene's sunny voice felt a little jarring and at the same time comforting and familiar.

"Hey Mom."

"Are things good with you and Tracy?"

"Yeah, I'm actually in her room, she's right here."

Tracy lay back on the bed mortified and pulled the sheet up over her face.

Robin chuckled and covered the phone receiver with her hand.

"It's not a picture phone, silly. She can't see you."

Removing her hand and turning back to the call with her mother, Robin said, "She's got the bed sheet up over her head as if you can see her."

Tracy pulled the sheet down and shook her head back and forth. She picked up the other pillow and threw it at Robin who caught it and laughed.

"Mom, I can't stay on long. Is there something you called about?"

"I just wanted to ask you one question, Robbie."

"Okay, what?"

"Have you told her you love her?"

Robin looked at the phone and sighed at it. She paused and took a deep breath.

"Not yet," she said.

"Why not, for godsakes?"

"Mom, that's two questions and, I'm sorry to say, that's all the time we have for you today. Thank you for your call."

Wendy spoke over Robin and said, "Tell her, Robbie. Tell her."

"Okay, Mom, bye now."

190

Returning to the bed, Robin drew Tracy into her arms.

"What was that all about?" Tracy asked.

Robin pulled Tracy closer and looked deeply into her soft green eyes, hoping she was doing the right thing.

"Did you hear me say 'not yet'?"

"Yes?"

"Can you guess what she asked me?"

"I hope it wasn't about whether we've had sex."

"No." She spoke slowly now. "She asked me if I'd told you yet that I love you because, well, I do."

Robin let the words sink in.

Tracy's mouth curled up into a smile.

"Well, I guess that's rather fortunate for me since I love you too. I've been wanting to tell you ever since that first phone call last month, but I was worried that things were still too new with us and I didn't know how you'd react."

Robin found Tracy's ear.

"This is how. I love you Tracy Patterson. I'm in love with you. It's the most intense and wonderful feeling I've ever felt."

A tear rolled down Tracy's cheek.

"I've been in love with you for so long and I spent so much time running away from it."

Tracy tucked her head into Robin's bare chest and began to cry softly. Robin kissed her neck.

"Shh, baby, don't cry. It's all good now. All the icky stuff is behind us."

She held Tracy and wiped away her tears with reassuring words. Then she kissed Tracy's mouth and moved on top placing a thigh between her legs. Tracy let out a sharp breath.

"If it's okay with you," Robin said as she began to touch Tracy's nipple, "I'd like to have sex with the woman I love."

Tracy moaned "yes" and pulled Robin closer.

Some time later, Tracy glanced at the clock next to the bed and saw that it was a few minutes after noon. She sat up in bed with a start.

"Robin, I've got to get ready. I have my first appointment with Professor Coolidge in less than an hour."

Robin groaned and lay on her back with one arm covering her eyes.

"It's very difficult for me to reconcile the fact that there's a whole life we have to live outside of this bed."

Tracy stood up and leaned over to give Robin a quick peck on her lips.

"I know, sweetie, but there is and we've got to get to it. I was thinking that maybe you'd come with me and we could both tell Professor Coolidge our good news."

Robin sat up and looked at Tracy.

"That's a good idea. She probably spent the summer obsessing about your choice of seating in the seminar last semester."

"You know, she asked me about that," Tracy said as she rifled through a still unpacked suitcase for some clothes.

"Did you tell her?"

Robin was putting on the clothes that were lying rumpled on the floor.

"No. I was afraid that if I opened up, I'd lose it completely and not be able to finish the semester. She seemed to accept that and we left it there."

CHAPTER NINETEEN

While most of her colleagues dreaded the beginning of another school year, Patty Coolidge relished it. She loved how Boston rejuvenated itself each September with the return of thousands of young college students, their U-Haul trucks clogging the narrow streets and their bodies crowding the aisles of hardware stores and supermarkets. She knew she could count on at least three more weeks of summer after school began, with the bonus of cooler nights when she and Jenny could walk along the path on the Cambridge side of the Charles River and watch as the sun set into the glistening water.

There was still good weather for sailing on the weekends, which gave them the opportunity to take the boat out and head into Boston harbor. As the early fall winds picked up, it took a bit more skill and strength to navigate, but after so many years spent on the water, they managed pretty well.

What she really looked forward to was October, when they headed up to the house in Vermont and looked out over a breathtaking vista of bright red, yellow, and orange leaves. They knew which local farm stand sold the most delicious cider and which had the best apples for pies. They bought pumpkins for baking and knobby gourds for decoration. There was no better place in the fall than Vermont.

Patty sat at her desk reading email. She was back in her teaching drag, a short sleeved mint green blouse and cream-colored slacks and blazer. There was a department meeting and reception for new graduate students at four and she knew she'd have to establish authority over her teaching assistants on day one. It was important to make it clear from the beginning that she held their future in her hands. Otherwise they'd neglect their teaching assistant responsibilities and slack off on producing the research she needed from them. She was scheduled to submit two journal papers for publication this year and to present a third at a conference. She needed as much help as she could get to meet all her deadlines.

Today was the first day of classes and Patty was ready to begin with a new crop of freshmen slouching expectantly in their seats as she took command of the lecture hall. She wondered if she'd again find a jewel among them as she had last year with Tracy Patterson. It was unlikely. Students like Tracy came along only a few times in one's career. She was looking forward to their first weekly check in at one.

Tracy had emailed all her research assignments over the summer. Everything Patty received was thorough and insightful. She wondered if she could keep Tracy at Adams for grad school. It would be a thrill to work with her as she proceeded toward her PhD. But when she thought about it fairly, she knew that Tracy deserved to be in one of the top programs in the country and Patty's own selfish needs shouldn't stand in her way.

She thought back to her conversation with Tracy last spring right before finals week. She'd watched with great disappointment when the sweet passion and excitement between Tracy and Robin Greene turned into ice-cold silence as the two of them continued to sit side by side, but with their bodies turned slightly away from one another. And then there was the day that Tracy changed her seat. That was when Patty had intervened, telling herself that she needed to make sure that her star research assistant was all right, when in reality she was actually dying of curiosity to find out what had happened between the two of them.

She smiled as she recalled Tracy turning her down flat, just the way she had rejected Tracy's sexual advances earlier last fall. She'd been just as disappointed at Tracy's refusal to discuss her issues with Robin as Tracy had been to be told that Patty was not going to begin an affair. And

194

although her focus and interest in Tracy had grown over the past year, she still only thought of her as a brilliant mentee and, possibly in the future, a friend.

She wished for Tracy the same happiness that she had found with Jenny.

Again, she smiled to herself, this time sadly. Happiness. That had been their project assignment. Patty had been very deliberate in her choice. And when she read their paper she actually felt their happiness and, yes even their love, radiating up from the pages. What could have happened to change that? Maybe today Tracy would be ready to talk.

Three soft knocks on her door signaled Tracy's arrival. Patty called out to her to come in and Tracy entered her office, a big smile on her face. There was only one word to describe how she looked—radiant. Her skin glowed and the designer jeans and pale yellow, cotton, short sleeved blouse she wore added to her overall sunniness. Patty was a little embarrassed at the thought that entered her mind as she beheld Tracy. *She looks like someone who's been having mind-blowing sex.*

"Tracy!" she said. "How great to see you. How was your summer?"

Patty stood and offered her hand to Tracy who took it. She was still a little reticent to hug Tracy given her student's original plans for seduction.

Relaxed and poised, Tracy sat across the desk from the professor and crossed her legs.

"Well, Professor, my summer was very bad and then very good."

"Okay," Patty said smiling, "let's start with the very good part, kind of like that saying about eating dessert first."

Tracy looked down at her lap for a second and then raised her head to face Patty eye-to-eye, a big smile on her face.

"I'm pleased to report that I have a girlfriend and I couldn't be happier."

"Oh, Tracy. What good news." *Well*, thought Patty, *that explains the blinding glow emanating from her.* She wondered if this had happened in North Carolina and she had a momentary pang of regret on behalf of Robin.

"Is she back home?" she asked, hoping the answer was not yes.

"No Professor, she's right here at Adams and I'd like you to meet her." Tracy stood and went to the door, opening it a crack. "You can come in now," she called in a singsong voice.

Patty held her breath, and almost crossed her fingers.

The door opened wide and Robin walked in smiling. She had the same glow as Tracy even though she was dressed in her usual grubby college student-faded jeans and t-shirt.

"Hi Professor, surprise!"

Patty stood up from her chair and began to laugh and nod her head, relieved that the two of them had finally succeeded in coming together. She couldn't contain her own happiness for them.

"Hello Robin. I was hoping you'd be the one to walk through that door. I'm so glad you did."

Robin and Tracy stood facing Professor Coolidge holding hands.

"Well, I know you guys need to have a real meeting, so I'll be going," Robin said.

She turned to Tracy.

"See you soon?" she said.

"Oh yes," Tracy responded and then leaned forward to kiss Robin goodbye. The kiss lasted a little longer than intended.

Patty beamed at them and then remembered who she was and where they all were. She loudly cleared her throat and they pulled apart.

"Sorry Professor," Tracy said.

"Ah young love." Patty said with a sigh and then turned to Robin pointing and grinning, "You! Get out of here now before this meeting devolves from PG to X rated."

Robin smiled. "Professor Coolidge, I am proud to report to you that on the subject of happiness…" She paused and then announced dramatically as she raised her hand to her forehead, "Mission accomplished!" She saluted.

As Robin strode out of the office, Tracy sat back down across from Patty's desk.

"Well, Tracy, I'd say you've started off the semester quite well, don't you think?"

Tracy blushed and nodded.

Patty picked up some notes she'd been making for her journal article and pointed them at Tracy.

"Okay, now let's get to work."

CHAPTER TWENTY

Two weeks apart and Tracy was dreading it. She vowed that after the upcoming Christmas break, she and Robin would never again be separated for this length of time. She couldn't handle it. Even through all of their ups and downs during the past year, Robin had become almost a part of her, and when there was physical or emotional distance between them, she felt less than whole, less like herself.

They had both spent the short Thanksgiving holiday in New York. Robin took her to watch the Macy's Thanksgiving Day parade where they stood crowded with a million other people on Central Park West, sharing a thermos of hot chocolate that Wendy had prepared for them. She and Robin snuggled together as they watched the debut of the giant balloons of Barney the Dinosaur and the Cat in the Hat. They were like little kids; Robin got all excited at the sight of Superman, and Tracy called out to Santa when his float rode by at the end of the parade.

Wendy, David, and Adam had welcomed her as part of the family and she even had a chance to mend fences with TJ and Sophia after the disastrous night last spring. TJ had begun to call her "the exception to the Princess Pact" which Robin said was about the best she could hope for.

Now with Christmas vacation coming up, she would be on her own again in Durham until right before New Year's Eve when she would join Robin back in New York for the rest of their break. Her parents had not been pleased with this arrangement, but after all the unhappiness they had witnessed last summer, they gave in.

"So how many hours are there in two weeks?" Robin asked one night as they sat on the bed studying for finals.

Tracy looked up from the laptop balanced on her crossed legs, her half-finished paper for Abnormal Psych on the screen.

"Too many. This is going to be torture."

"Hey," Robin said as she caressed Tracy's chin, "it'll go by fast, you'll see. Look at the bright side. At least this time we get to have phone sex. I'm assuming that ban has been lifted, right?"

Tracy nodded and smiled sadly.

"Might be the only thing that gets me through, except if they kick me out of the house after I come out to them; then I won't even be able to call you."

"Baby, that's not gonna happen."

"You haven't met my mother. It's not like it is with your parents, where everything you do is okay."

Robin positioned herself behind Tracy and put her arms around her waist, laying her head on Tracy's shoulder.

"It might be a bit unpleasant, but you'll tell them a few days before you leave so you won't have to stick around for too much bad stuff."

Tracy lifted the computer off her lap and snuggled her back into Robin's body, finding the comfort it always provided.

A week later Tracy's packed Louis Vuitton roller bag sat in the middle of her room. Angie stood at Tracy's desk leafing through the reading pile she was taking in her carry-on.

Robin came through the door, an army duffle on her shoulder. She was driving Tracy to the airport.

"Ready when you are babe. Your plane leaves in ninety minutes."

"Very eclectic reading, Ms. Patterson," Angie said holding up a book, an academic journal, and a magazine. "We have December's *Vogue*, the *Journal of Humanistic Psychology* (I guess in case the *Vogue* isn't too exciting), and a copy of *Curious Wine* that I loaned you."

Robin chuckled. "That's my girl." She paused. "Oh, hey, I hear the author of *Curious Wine* is up for the Nobel Prize in Literature."

Tracy took her reading material from Angie, walked over to Robin and bopped her gently on the head with it.

"Robin Greene, it would do you a world of good to read a sweet little lesbian romance for a change," she said. "You, my love, are a reading snob."

"You really are," said Angie as she walked over to Robin. "What's in *your* reading pile? Wait let me guess, Sartre and de Beauvoir?"

"If you must know, yes," said Robin. "And I'm kind of interested in Alice Munro's new short stories and a book by V. S. Naipul that I read about."

Angie groaned in response.

"I'll take Lane and Diana from *Curious Wine* over that any day."

Tracy zipped up her light brown, soft, leather carry-on and wheeled the roller bag over to Robin who took it from her.

"Come on, my cute little literature snob," said Tracy, kissing Robin quickly on the lips, "I wouldn't want to miss my plane and not be able to come out to my parents."

#

As Tracy walked off the escalator toward the baggage claim area at the Raleigh-Durham airport, she looked around for her father who was nowhere to be found. Then she heard someone call her name and turned around to see Bradley Farrell walking toward her. Sometimes it was a little unsettling how much Bradley looked like his mother. He had Millicent's gray-blue eyes, long turned up nose, and wavy medium brown hair. He stood tall in his brown bomber jacket and faded jeans.

"Bradley," she said and hugged him when he got near. "I was looking for Daddy. What are you doing here?"

"I had to drop something by your house for my momma and found out that you were on your way home today, so I volunteered to come get you and save Billy the trip."

"What a nice surprise. How long will you be home?"

Bradley took Tracy's roller bag from her and led her out of the busy terminal to his car.

"Only through the twenty-sixth and then I'm going back up to Pennsylvania to visit with Mary Ellen's family. I wanted to bring her down for Christmas but I'm not sure Momma's quite ready to be civilized."

Tracy thought back to that day at the beach house when Bradley had hung up on Millicent. The searing memory of standing in shock as Millicent declared that she and Bradley should get married and live back in Durham hit her like a slap in the face.

Bradley opened the passenger door of his blue Ford Escort so Tracy could get in and then stowed her bag in the back seat. He drove through the airport and out onto the highway toward Durham.

"So your momma still hasn't accepted your relationship with Mary Ellen? How long have you been dating her?"

"It's been almost two years. You know we plan on living together in Philadelphia after graduation."

"Does your momma know that?"

"Yes, but she still thinks we're going to break up before then. You know what they say about denial, not just a river in Egypt."

Tracy smiled. "You know, Bradley, they've had an agenda for a while to get you and me together."

Tracy noticed Bradley's expression change to one of concern, his mouth turned down and his head lowered.

"This is not something you're a part of, is it?"

Tracy turned in her seat to face him.

"God no," she said. "I'm seeing someone back at school just like you."

His smile returned. "Girl, you've been holding out on me. Who is the lucky guy?"

"Bradley, it's not a guy, it's a girl." She paused. "I'm gay."

She watched his face closely as he took in the information. He looked puzzled for a few seconds and then he turned to her, smiled and nodded his head.

"Well aren't you a big surprise, Miss Tracy. Did ol' Brett Jamison scare you away from men for good?"

Tracy breathed out to signal her annoyance at this comment.

"Oh c'mon now, I'm just teasing you." He lightly swatted her arm with his hand.

"Bradley, Brett and I were never really a couple. We're both gay and we used each other as a cover in high school. It's not something I'm proud of now, but I understand why we felt the need to do it."

"Wow, Brett too, huh? But not Jeff Jordan, right? Big football hero, strong silent type."

"Jeff and Brett *are* a couple. They've been together since junior year."

Bradley turned fully to face Tracy.

"Nooooooo."

Tracy put her hand on Bradley's face and turned it toward the front.

"Bradley, as much as I don't want to come out to my parents during this visit, I'm not so sure I want to avoid it by dying in a car crash. Please watch the road."

"You're actually gonna tell them? Do you think that's wise? I mean, look at the fuss my momma's making over Mary Ellen just being Catholic."

Tracy sighed. "That's the plan. I'm determined to stop hiding. Next time I come back, I want it to be with Robin."

"That's your...your?"

"Girlfriend."

"Wow, I gotta give you points for bravery, that's for sure."

They were both quiet for a few minutes. Tracy wanted to tell Bradley more about Robin, but he hadn't asked and she wondered if maybe he had as much information as he could deal with in one sitting. His expression was thoughtful and serious as he sped the car down the highway.

"You wanna hear something weird, Tracy?" he began. "I've often wondered about my momma. I mean, she and Daddy have lived apart for all these years, only seeing each other on holidays, if that. Oh, she's got her garden club and other things, but I think she uses the excuse of still being married, to I don't know, shield herself. And because she's so closed off, it makes her less accepting of the choices that other people make—like me, for instance."

He looked straight ahead, frowning and shaking his head.

"I just don't even know if she's ever been happy, like truly happy. I could be crazy, but I've often thought that maybe she'd be happier in a relationship with another woman. The only time I've even seen her remotely content is when she's among women."

Tracy sat stunned. She felt her face flush and she instantly looked down at her lap. What could she possibly say to this? He was completely on target about Millicent, and yet, she could never reveal what she knew and, least of all, how she knew it. She sat with her hands clasped together in her lap trying to slow her racing heartbeat and compose herself before she spoke.

"I don't know," she said at last, "you could be right, but I suspect that it doesn't much matter. It's not like your momma's gonna make any big changes in her life anyway. Millicent's been Millicent for as long as I can remember. She's very similar to my momma. They care far too much about how things look to other people to ever go out on a limb about anything."

As Bradley steered the car off the highway, he nodded in agreement.

"I suspect you're right."

#

Ten days later, Tracy woke to the sound of her bedroom phone ringing. She and Robin had kept to their pledge that theirs be the first voices they heard in the morning and the last before they went to sleep.

"Hey, welcome to my big day," she said in a sleepy voice.

"Yeah," said Robin. "How are you feeling about it?"

Tracy lay on her back stretching her body awake and yawning.

"Like I'm just wanting to get it over with. I'm sick of obsessing about it. How are you doing this morning, sweetie?"

"I'm just thinking about you. Now it's me who's obsessing. You know I'll be near the phone all day if you need me."

"Mmmm, I have a wonderful girlfriend, you know that?" she said.

"God do I miss waking up with you. I've gotten really used to someone kissing my neck in the morning."

"When do you think you're gonna tell them?"

"You *are* obsessing," Tracy said as she sat up in bed. "It's not like you to ignore a remark about kissing my neck."

"Sorry, I hope I'm not making you more anxious."

"Don't worry, you're not. I'm gonna tell them after dinner tonight."

Tracy heard a soft knock on her door.

"Hold on a sec," she told Robin.

"Yes? I'm awake," she called out.

The door opened and her mother stood there in her fuzzy white terry cloth robe with yellow piping.

"Who are you talking to so early?" she asked.

"Robin. What's up Momma?"

"I was hoping you could do me a favor today and return some gifts over at the Emerald Village Mall. I've got a $100 gift certificate for Saks that you can have for your troubles."

Tracy's eyes were wide.

"Seeing as how I would have done it without the bribe, I'd say you've got yourself a deal."

"All right. You might want to get an early start. You won't be the only one on the returns line two days after Christmas." Her voice brightened. "Oh and Sue Ann Tyson tells me there's an extremely handsome young man from UNC who's at the Macy's counter. You may want to wear something nice."

Tracy rolled her eyes.

"I don't think so, Momma."

"Well, I'll let you get back to your phone call," her mother said as she closed the door behind her.

Tracy put the phone back to her ear just as Robin began to speak.

"I finally get to hear the voice of the famous Luanne Patterson, always on the lookout for a handsome young man for her beautiful daughter."

"No, she's always on the lookout for a handsome young man for her daughter who bites her nails," Tracy said. "Well, after today, there'll be no more of that kind of talk because she won't be talking to me at all."

"Don't worry, sweetie. You'll get through this. By the way, I've seen how you shop. You're going to burn through that hundred bucks in about five minutes."

"Well even if it is just five minutes, I can't think of a better form of therapy today."

#

On her way home from shopping, Tracy slowed down as she passed Millicent Farrell's house and noticed that Bradley's car wasn't in the driveway. She recognized Millicent's red Acura in its usual spot in front of the garage and pulled in behind it.

"Tracy, I'm surprised to see you. To what do I owe the honor of your visit?" Millicent drawled sarcastically as she led Tracy through the entranceway into the living room. Tracy reasoned that this greeting was a bit deserved. After all, she'd been making a point of avoiding her former lover ever since she'd gone away to college.

The Farrell home was impeccably decorated in shades of slate blue, mauve, and white, with a large oriental rug adorning most of the living room's polished hardwood floor. Millicent gestured for Tracy to take a seat on the blue and white patterned couch and sat down about a foot away from her.

"Can I get you some tea or something cold to drink?"

"I'm fine, thank you," Tracy said with a short wave of her hand. "Millicent, I came over to talk to you about something I'm about to tell my parents later today and I need you to know about it first. I'm going to tell them that I'm gay and that I'm in a relationship with another woman."

Shock and dismay registered on Millicent's face. Her gray-blue eyes darkened with something Tracy could only describe as anger.

"Tracy, have you gone mad? Why on earth would you think that such a thing is necessary? It will only bring so much misery to your poor parents."

Tracy swallowed. She'd known this would not be easy. It was a kind of dress rehearsal for what she was going to do later. But there was no

206

avoiding it; she needed to have this conversation with Millicent first. And she knew that the only way to get them both through it was to be as kind as possible.

"Millicent, I know this is not easy for you to understand. But I've made a decision to stop hiding, especially from my parents. I love them and I want my relationship with them to be built on honesty, not on a pile of lies. And I have no intention of concealing my relationship with my girlfriend Robin like it's something shameful. I just won't live like that anymore."

Millicent looked down and ran the fingers of both hands through her hair, a gesture of frustration that Tracy had seen before.

"Well then," she said in a tight voice, "if you are so adamant about this why come over here to tell me?"

"There are two reasons. First, I want to reassure you of something. I will never tell my parents or Bradley, for that matter, what happened between us. I would never make that decision for you. I didn't want you to hear about this from Momma and worry that I had said something that could violate your privacy."

Millicent turned to look at Tracy.

"All right," she said. "I do appreciate that and, you're right, I would have worried about it."

Tracy nodded and continued.

"The second thing is that I know this will not be easy for Momma. I'm hoping over time that changes, but at least for now, it'll be difficult. I wanted to ask you to be there for her. She's going to need somebody to talk to besides Daddy. You're her best friend and she really cares about what you think."

Millicent's eyes were dark again.

"Tracy, I hope you're not asking me to convince her that this is all okay."

Tracy took a deep breath, trying to control her anger. Millicent was not making it easy for her to remain kind, that was for sure. Here was a woman who had made love with her dozens of times but who was ready to condemn her for loving women. There was just no limit to her capacity for self-deception.

Now it was Tracy whose voice came out strained.

"Millicent, of course what I want most is for Momma to have someone she can turn to. But I don't know what there is to be gained by you (and I have to say, you of all people) fanning the flames of disapproval. Yes, you and I have made very different choices in our lives, but under all that, we are the same." Unable to hold back her feelings any longer, she added, "and you know exactly what I mean."

Millicent looked at Tracy and then turned her head up toward the ceiling. "I used to think we were the same, but not any longer." Her voice was soft and haughty. "You would be much better off if you would live a normal life and take care of other things on the side."

Tracy thought about her relationship with Robin. It was the most wonderful and authentic thing she'd ever experienced. The idea that Millicent was urging her to push it off into the shadows and live some kind of pretend life enraged her. Nothing would ever cause her to do that. She would defend and celebrate their love no matter what anyone said or did. She knew that what she needed to say now might turn Millicent against her forever, but she was so upset by this last remark that she no longer cared.

As she stood up to leave, she looked down at Millicent sitting on the couch.

"Millicent, in my view, *you* would be much better off if you let yourself experience the kind of love and happiness that I have with Robin.

Even though I am furious with you right now, I really do wish that for you one day. You can still open yourself up to it. It's not too late."

Millicent stood up from the couch to her full height, her body rigid. "You have no right, young lady, to sit in judgment of me."

Tracy turned away and began to walk toward the door.

"Goodbye," she said. "I'll show myself out."

#

All through dinner Tracy tried to keep up a brave front. It was not easy to sit calmly and discuss her shopping trip or listen to her mother's local updates about people she cared very little about. Although she wasn't hungry, she forced herself to eat enough so that her father wouldn't notice and think she was sliding back into last summer's depression.

As her mother stood to clear the table, Tracy spoke up.

"Momma, do you think that could wait a few minutes. I wanted to talk to you and Daddy about something and I need your full attention."

"I can listen to you while I clean up," her mother said.

"No Momma, I'd really prefer you sit."

Her mother sighed and returned to her seat.

"As you wish," she said with resignation.

Tracy looked at both of them as they sat at the small, round oak kitchen table; her mother with her honey colored hair pinned up in a clip, her periwinkle long sleeved blouse tucked into midnight blue slacks; her father in a gray cotton cardigan, white t-shirt, and black twill pants; his thinning, light brown hair parted on the side. She took a deep breath and placed her hands in front of her on the table.

"I hope you both know how much I love you. And because of that I want us to have the best relationship possible. What I mean is I want to have the most honest relationship with you that I can."

She snuck a quick look at them. Her mother's face was a question and her father's showed concern. She wondered if he was looking at her the way he looked at his patients.

"Actually," she said, "I'm the one who hasn't been honest with you. For the past few years, I've hidden the most important parts of my life from you and led you to believe things that weren't true. But that all ends right now."

She caught her breath for a second and worked hard to keep her gaze steady. She looked at each of them.

"Momma, Daddy, I'm gay. I have been since high school. I've dated boys and I've dated girls and it quickly became very clear to me which I preferred."

Her father looked down at the table and she could hear him breathing.

"No," her mother said in an angry whisper. "You are mistaken, Tracy. This cannot be."

"Momma, yes…"

"No!" she was louder now. "I won't permit it. W-w-why, you just haven't met the right boy yet. You've been too stubborn about not dating and opening yourself up to the possibilities."

"Momma, that's not true." Tracy leaned forward toward her mother hoping maybe she could make her understand. "Just as strange and foreign as it would feel for you to think about other women the way you think about men, that's how it is for me with boys. My attraction is to other women, not men."

Her mother looked at her father.

"Billy, please don't just sit there saying nothing like this is one of your sessions. Tell the girl that this isn't true. It's not real. I mean, look at her. She's pretty, feminine. She's not one of those… tough, truck driving types."

Tracy's father looked up and spoke in a quiet voice.

"Luanne, it just doesn't work that way, I'm afraid. There are no types. Most people these days seem to think that this is something you're born with, not something you become."

This was now their conversation with Tracy as the audience.

"Well then set her up with that Doctor Peters or someone, maybe a man. Aren't there therapies that can change this?"

Tracy gasped and was near tears.

"Momma, no! That's not even true." She looked at her father. "Tell her Daddy."

"She's right," Billy said with a sigh.

"And besides," Tracy continued, her voice stronger, "even if it were possible, I don't want to change. I'm the happiest I've ever been. I have a wonderful relationship back up at school with Robin. It started at the beginning of the semester."

Her mother sat back with her arms crossed over her chest and looked at her husband.

"You insisted she go up there for college when she could have gone anywhere down here. Now you see what you've done. They've convinced her that anything goes, that she can be with a girl, a boy or, heaven knows, what else. This would never have happened had she gone to Duke like she should have."

"Momma, that's not so," Tracy said, refusing to be left out of the conversation. "I was gay before I set foot up north; I just wasn't honest about it. That's all that's changed."

Her mother finally turned to her.

"How can that be? You were with Brett almost the entire time you were in high school."

Tracy shook her head. "No, Momma, that was all an act. It was one of the many lies I told back then to hide myself from you and Daddy."

She heard her father sigh and turned to him.

"I'm truly sorry for that. It was very wrong to lie, but at the time I just didn't think there was any other way. Now I know better."

"Oh no you don't, missy," said her mother, her voice now angry and louder. "Not by a long shot, you don't. Did you think this was going to be easy for me? Do you think anyone here is going to understand or accept this?"

Her mother rose from the table and picked up her plate.

"I have heard all that I care to hear about this." She turned her back to Tracy and walked to the sink.

Tracy looked at her father, pleading. He put his hand over her wrist.

"I think that's enough for now, honey. Give your momma and me some time with this. It's not an easy thing. But, I want you to know that you are still my daughter and I do love you."

A tear rolled down Tracy's cheek as her father leaned over and kissed her forehead.

As her mother stood at the sink, her soft crying could be heard over the sound of running water. Tracy rose from her chair, walked out of the kitchen and ran up the stairs to call Robin.

#

Two days later she was in the passenger seat of her father's Ford Taurus headed to the airport, relieved at the prospect of finally feeling Robin's arms around her. Things had remained tense with her mother, who spoke to her only when necessary and said nothing more about their conversation. Her father didn't say much either, but he'd been more

212

reassuring, hugging her a few times and making a point of coming in to say goodnight to her before heading off to bed. She had no idea what the next step in this process should be and was resigned to wait and see if time alone could work its magic.

As she sat quietly in the car with her leather bag at her feet, her father placed his hand over hers affectionately. He finally spoke as the first highway signs for the airport came into view.

"I bet you're relieved to be gettin' out of Dodge, huh?"

Surprised at his opening, it took her a few seconds to respond.

"Yes and no," she said. "I hate leaving Momma in such a state with so much unresolved between us. Do you think it'll be okay at some point?"

"I do, honey." He patted her hand. "You know your momma, she has a certain set of expectations about life and when something gets in the way of all that it knocks her off kilter. You leave her to me, okay?"

"Thanks Daddy. I really am grateful for your support and your love. You really made all of this more bearable for me."

Her father was quiet for a moment and then he turned to her.

"You mentioned the other day that you had somebody back up at school, your friend, Robin, did you say?"

Tracy felt giddy. He actually wanted to talk about this.

"Yes," she replied unable to hide the eagerness in her voice.

"Well, why don't you tell me about her? What do you like about her?"

"Oh Daddy I'm so glad you want to know. She's truly wonderful and so kind and sweet to me. I think I've told you before that she's a writer. She's in this very prestigious program at Adams. I don't know if you've ever heard of Joe Donovan, but he runs it."

Her father steered the car onto the airport service road.

"Oh yes, he writes those books set in Boston, doesn't he? I read one once. It was very good."

"You know, Robin would never admit it, but I think she could be the best writer in that program. Joe's said some really positive things to her. She's very talented. And she's smart and funny and fearless, really fearless. She cares about so many things. She runs a writing group in Boston for homeless teenagers."

Her father nodded.

"That's really good. Gives those kids an outlet for all their pain."

Yes. I guess the most wonderful thing is that she inspires me to be the best person I can be. I think we do that for one another. Daddy, this relationship is like nothing I've ever experienced in my life. It's hard to explain, but I feel like I finally know who I am."

PART II

1997

CHAPTER TWENTY-ONE

As Robin walked up College Avenue from their apartment toward campus, she noticed a few light green buds peeking through the bare branches of the tall elm trees that lined the street. She sighed as she climbed the hill up from Adams House Circle past the athletic fields. Senior year was supposed to be easy, a coast to the finish line. But their senior year had been a slog.

It began horribly in early September the day after she and Tracy celebrated their two-year anniversary. Angie came back from a visit to Harvard looking like she'd seen a ghost. She was in a fog, her eyes glassy and expressionless, her face drawn and pale. She sat saying nothing for ten minutes while Robin and Tracy tried to coax her to speak. Finally, over the next few hours, a few words trickled out.

"Over."

"Ended it."

"Leaving."

"New York."

"Maria."

Tracy sat with her arms around Angie, trying to get her to tell them more.

"Did something happen with Nicky? Did she break up with you?"

Angie could only nod. In the days ahead, as Angie spoke a few short sentences at a time, they were able to piece together the full story.

Nicky had come back to Boston for a day just to tell Angie the news. She was leaving Harvard and would be finishing her degree at Columbia. During that previous summer, Nicky had re-connected with her old

217

girlfriend, Maria, who'd been her first love. They had originally met when Nicky started playing basketball with the girls in Maria's neighborhood. After Maria broke things off to be with a guy, Nicky left for Harvard determined to forget her.

Now, four years later, Maria had finally accepted herself as a lesbian and wanted them to be together. Nicky had made excuses to Angie all summer about why she couldn't see her, and now Angie finally understood the reason.

As the story took shape, Robin became more and more livid. She'd never liked Nicky much, but this sudden and unexpected kick in the teeth that completely destroyed her best friend sent her into overdrive. It was only Tracy's intercession that prevented Robin from getting into her car, driving to New York and going after Nicky.

"Honey, it wouldn't accomplish a damn thing for you to go and confront her," Tracy said as she put her hands on Robin's shoulders. "It would just end in one or both of you getting physically hurt and I'm not gonna let you do that, especially if I'm four hours away when it happens. Besides I need you here with Angie. She needs both of us now."

"I could send TJ after her. She's always had a thing for Angie. She'd pulverize Nicky."

"Robin, no," Tracy said. "Don't get TJ mixed up in this. The last thing she needs is to be arrested for assault. She finally has a good job at that youth shelter. And you know that Nicky's family has all kinds of money and power. They could easily send TJ back to the streets, or even worse, to jail."

In the end, Tracy had been right. Angie did need both of them to get her through the year. For the first month, she never left the apartment. They couldn't get her to eat much and she cried every night. Robin, Tracy, and Barbara took turns lying in bed and holding her so she could get some sleep.

Not knowing what to do, Tracy finally talked to Professor Coolidge who enlisted a therapist friend to begin seeing Angie. She came to the apartment a few times, until Angie was able to venture out to her office in Cambridge. By midterms, Angie was back in class a few days a week and was able to attend to her responsibilities as student body president. She got through the semester because Robin wrote all her papers and Tracy sat in on her classes and took notes.

After that, they had to get her through her law school applications. Again, Robin wrote and Tracy collected the necessary documents, including recommendations. Luckily, Angie had taken the LSATs before all this happened and scored in the ninety-ninth percentile.

While this was going on, Tracy was applying to psychology PhD programs and working on a number of research projects for Professor Coolidge. She'd already had her name included on two published papers in psych journals as third and fourth author. This year's projects, if successful, would push her up to second, right behind Patty Coolidge. Still, she confided to Robin her worry that she didn't have what it would take to become a skilled clinician, with the ability to bring insight and clarity to other peoples' lives. Despite her efforts to reassure Tracy, Robin knew that her doubts lingered.

Robin kept writing and took classes in subjects that she wanted to write about or that she thought all writers should know. She'd mastered Greek mythology and studied most of Shakespeare. She took courses in religious studies, learning more about Judaism and acquiring a basic knowledge of Christianity, Islam, and Buddhism. She took a seminar on the Holocaust and studied the Civil War and the slave trade in history classes. She tried her hand at writing poetry and tackled *Finnegan's Wake* in a literature course.

Last year, Joe Donovan had convinced his publisher, Elizabeth Morrison, the head of Morrison Publishing, to review a manuscript of Robin's short story collection. To Robin's amazement, Morrison took her on, setting forth a flurry of legal and financial activity that Robin was completely unprepared for. Luckily her father, who regularly negotiated with recording artists for his record label, stepped in to ensure that Robin's contract was fair. He then worked with Joe to find Robin a literary agent who could represent her going forward.

Once the legalities were out of the way, she was assigned an editor, a young woman who was only a few years older than she was. It was one thing to take feedback from Joe, but to have to listen to someone she hardly knew or trusted had been incredibly frustrating.

"Her notes and comments are all about business and marketing, not about the quality of the writing," she complained to Joe.

"Robin, this is the game," he said with a hint of exasperation in his voice. "Unless you want your work to sit in a drawer and never see the light of day, you've got to listen to this woman."

It had not been easy to give in, but in the end she did. The book, which she had titled, *The Streets and the Pier*, a collection of short fiction about homeless teens, was due to be released on April fifteenth. Elizabeth had pulled some strings at the *Times* to get a review in the Sunday book section.

Robin was now having trouble sleeping, sitting up nights thinking about that review and how it could make or break her. Tracy was also having trouble sleeping, worrying about getting into grad school. Their plan was to move to New York if Tracy could get in to either Columbia or NYU.

"Tracy, you need to calm down," Robin said one night when they both couldn't sleep. "Coolidge knows the guy at Columbia and she basically told him that you were the psychology messiah. You read the glowing recommendation she wrote."

"I don't know how much weight that will carry. Besides, there could be dozens of other applicants, many from Ivy League colleges, with the same kind of glowing recommendations."

Robin had pulled her into her arms as they lay in bed.

"Not with your grades, your GREs, and all your publications." She kissed Tracy's neck and spoke seductively into her ear.

"I bet those other applicants don't sit around reading psych journals and lesbian romance novels. I bet they don't know Anna Wintour's favorite color this season like you do."

Tracy giggled. "It's tangerine," she said as she tickled Robin's sides.

Robin squirmed away laughing.

"See? You're infinitely more qualified than those stupid, straight, fashion-challenged Ivy Leaguers. They don't deserve to be in New York. Not the way they dress."

Tracy lay comfortably in her arms, her head resting on Robin's chest. In a few minutes, she was asleep.

#

Two weeks later, on the seventeenth of April, Robin walked down the two flights of stairs from their off-campus, third floor apartment to get the mail. Grad school decisions had been sent out on the fifteenth and it was likely that letters would be arriving today. Too nervous to look themselves, Tracy and Angie had put her in charge of collecting whatever envelopes arrived and then calling them in for an assessment of the thickness of each letter. Thin meant rejection and thick meant a likely acceptance.

221

There had been no thin envelopes yet. Angie was accepted to law schools at Georgetown, Boston College, and NYU. She still hadn't heard from Harvard. Tracy had also received a thick envelope from NYU, having been accepted into the psych PhD program. At least now, she and Robin knew they could move to New York. Even so, Tracy was still hoping to get into Columbia.

This was the second year they were renting this apartment in a house on a quiet street off College Avenue. It was a typical Boston triple-decker; three apartments stacked on top of each other inside a forest green-painted wood-shingled house with white trim. They were in a three bedroom unit, with Tracy and Robin sharing a room. The living room and kitchen were spacious, with hardwood floors and real wainscoting, while the bedrooms were on the small side. Their landlord, an elderly widow named Mrs. Connelly, lived on the second floor with her cat Timmy. Her son Jack and his wife Sheila lived below with their two bratty kids. Jack's creepy leers made Tracy and Angie uncomfortable. Mrs. Connelly, on the other hand, was very sweet. She brought them fresh-baked apple muffins and regularly invited them to attend mass with her at St. Paul's Church in Teele Square. On a few occasions Angie had actually accompanied her.

Robin grabbed the pile of mail from the box without looking at it. As she walked back up the steps wondering if today was the day, she almost ran right into Mrs. Connelly in her robe and slippers.

"Whoa, Mrs. Connelly, I'm so sorry. I wasn't looking where I was going. Tracy and Angie are waiting for grad school letters and we're all a little distracted."

Mrs. Connelly smiled.

"No harm done, dear. I was just going to get the mail myself."

Robin handed Mrs. Connelly the letters she had in her hands.

"If you hold onto this, I'll run down and get yours."

"Oh, Robin, that would be a big help. My legs are a little stiff today from the weather."

When Robin returned with three pieces of mail in her hand, Mrs. Connelly was still standing on the second floor landing holding onto the banister.

"Some very prestigious schools in this pile today," she said as she and Robin exchanged envelopes. "Harvard and Columbia."

Robin's face registered surprise and fear.

"Oh wow," she said and exhaled audibly. "Mrs. Connelly, I gotta go."

She took the flight of stairs two steps at a time.

A few minutes later, the three of them sat in their sparsely furnished living room. Robin carefully tore open the envelope from Harvard.

"Dear Ms. Antonelli," she read, "The Admissions Committee has reviewed your application and we are pleased to offer you a place in the first year class of Harvard Law School for the fall term of 1997."

There was stunned silence for a second and then Robin threw the letter into the air and let out a whoop.

"They are pleased! They are pleased! Angie, you got in!"

Tracy was already hugging Angie and Robin leaned forward to join.

"You're finally going to Harvard, Angie, congratulations."

Angie looked at her two friends with a small smile on her lips, her dark eyes full of gratitude. Robin had noticed that since the breakup with Nicky, Angie had dropped the broadest smiles from her repertoire and the light in her eyes had gone dim.

"I don't know what to say. This is as much your acceptance as it is mine. If it wasn't for the two of you…"

Angie lowered her head and began to cry, her hands covered her face.

Again, Tracy reached over to hug her.

"Angie, this is a day to celebrate. These were *your* grades, *your* LSATs, and *your* recommendations. You won that student election, not us. You interned in Congress, you worked for your cousin in the state legislature. You earned this. I'm just glad Harvard finally came to its senses."

Robin held a large square letter in her hand and raised it up.

"There's another envelope to open."

Angie looked up and wiped her eyes with her hands. Tracy breathed in and Angie took her hand.

Again, Robin opened the letter, this one with the Columbia University insignia. She removed the flat, unfolded letter from the large envelope and read it aloud.

"Dear Ms. Patterson, we are pleased to offer you admission to the doctoral program in psychology for the fall of 1997," Robin's voice was now louder and she read the words faster. "In light of your extraordinary qualifications, you have been awarded the Jeremy A. Rubin Fellowship of $25,000 for each year of study subject to your continued successful academic performance as set forth in the enclosed document."

Still grasping the letter, she leaned over and put her arms around Tracy who kept repeating, "Oh my God, oh my God."

Angie held on to Tracy from her other side and said, "Wow, Tracy, this is so great. They even gave you a fellowship."

Robin kissed Tracy and stood up.

"I bought champagne to celebrate."

"Robin, it's eleven o'clock in the morning," said Tracy.

"Oh you're right. I'll get the orange juice too. We'll have mimosas."

They were interrupted by the loud buzz of the downstairs doorbell.

"Hold on, let me see who this is." Robin walked to the apartment door and said "who's there" into the intercom.

The tinny voice on the other end said, "UPS, package for Greene."

Robin looked at Tracy and Angie and shook her head.

"I wasn't expecting…"

Tracy interrupted her.

"It must be your books. Remember, you were getting ten copies."

Robin opened the door and ran down, forgetting that she could have buzzed the delivery guy into the building. As she took the package and felt its weight, she noticed the return address of Morrison Publishing. She re-emerged into the apartment with the box wrapped in brown shipping paper.

She placed it on the coffee table and tore off the paper and then with some effort, pulled apart the taped cardboard underneath.

"Robin, don't hurt yourself, I'll get the scissors," said Tracy as she stood up.

"I got it," Robin said as she pulled on the last piece of packing tape.

There was bubble wrap on top and lining all four sides of the box. Robin grabbed at it wildly, trying to get to the books. Tracy stepped in and took hold of her hands.

"Please, before you rip a book apart. Let me."

In seconds, Tracy found the end of the sheet of bubble wrap and handed a piece to Robin.

"Here, play with this. It's great therapy."

There were pop, pop, popping noises now accompanying Tracy's effort to get to the books packed within. Finally, she lifted the last sheet and beheld three new hardback books sitting with their identical covers facing up. She gasped and pulled one out. Angie reached in for another.

225

The popping noises stopped and Robin leaned over Tracy to look at the book she held. Tracy again reached into the box and handed another copy to Robin. They all sat quietly staring at the books in their hands, reading the shiny paper jackets and leafing through the pages. Angie was absorbed in her copy, Robin's mouth was open, and tears rolled down Tracy's cheeks.

The front cover was a photo of the Christopher Street Pier taken at dusk with the Hudson River and the twinkling lights of New Jersey in the background. Silhouettes of kids with backpacks, hunched over in a huddle were visible. It was a sight that Robin had seen dozens of times. Above the picture against a blue background was the title, *The Streets and the Pier*, and below the photo, "Stories by Robin Greene."

#

The following Saturday, Robin and Tracy lay sleeping in each other's arms when the ringing phone jolted them awake. Robin groaned and reached over to the night table next to her, lifting the receiver and noting the time. Eight-thirty.

"Hello," she said with annoyance in her voice.

"Robin Greene?" the crisp female voice on the other end asked.

"Yeah," she replied with a yawn.

"This is Elizabeth Morrison of Morrison Publishing. Have you seen the *Times* book review yet? I don't know if it's available in Boston on a Saturday." Her tone was businesslike and to the point. The memory of Professor Coolidge's class-ending wrap up speeches sprang to mind.

Robin sat up.

"Ms. Morrison, is something wrong? Was the review bad?"

Tracy was now fully awake looking at Robin. She mouthed the question, "Elizabeth Morrison?" and Robin nodded.

"Well," Ms. Morrison's voice softened with a hint of playfulness, "I don't want to spoil anything for you. I'll have a copy messengered right over to your home. We'll be in touch on Monday when I'm back in the office. Goodbye for now."

Robin sat holding the phone.

"What did she say?" asked Tracy with some urgency in her voice.

"She's having the *Times* review messengered over here." Robin spoke like she was in a dream. "She sounds just like Professor Coolidge at the end of class."

Tracy ignored the last remark.

"Did she say what the review said? Was it good?"

"She said she didn't want to spoil anything." Robin was still in a trance.

Tracy took her hands.

"Well that could only be good news. She didn't sound angry or upset, did she?"

"No. I half expected her to start talking about Maslow and assign me a paper."

An hour later the downstairs buzzer rang and Robin let the messenger in the house. She opened the apartment door and waited. He handed her an eight-by-ten manila envelope addressed to her. She gave it to Tracy.

"Angie, Barbara," Tracy called out. "We have the *Times* review."

They sat around the square kitchen table as Tracy flipped the pages of the book review looking for the title of Robin's book. She found it on page ten.

"Here it is. The headline says, "Stories of Mean Families and Mean Streets." It's only one column long. The reviewer's name is Avery Parrish. I can't tell if that's a man or a woman. Does anyone recognize the name?"

Everyone shook their heads.

"Wait, here's a one-sentence bio." Tracy paused. "Oh," she said disappointed, "all it says is 'Avery Parrish writes young adult fiction.' That's not very helpful. Okay, here we go."

> *Pier 45 in lower Manhattan, also known as the Christopher Street Pier, has always had a place in New York's gay community. Back in the early years of gay liberation, it was a cruising spot for throngs of men. In more recent days, it has become the central gathering place for disaffected and homeless gay, lesbian and transgender youth, many who have been kicked out of homes all over the US.*
>
> *The twelve stories in Robin Greene's debut collection,* The Streets and the Pier, *not only pull tightly on your heartstrings as you read about the endless injustices these young people endure, they also fuel your sense of outrage at the families, the Church, the cops and the entire system of services supposedly set up to help them.*
>
> *At 21, only slightly older than the youth she brings to life in these stories, Greene is unsparing in her depiction of fathers who take physical revenge against the female lovers of their daughters, police who beat teens for sitting all day in McDonald's, and even at times the youth themselves, stealing and selling their bodies to get by.*
>
> *This is an important book from a fresh and original newcomer whose hard-hitting prose puts you right in the center of a crisis that no one seems to want to address. With every new story, Greene is shaking you awake and forcing you to not look away.*
>
> *If anyone can get all of us to pay attention, it's Robin Greene. Remember that name. This generation that is coming of age in its twenties now has a voice, and she is it.*

"The voice of our generation," Angie said, her mouth open and eyes wide. "Robin."

228

"Congratulations," Barbara spoke next.

Tracy opened her mouth to say something but then noticed that Robin sat slumped in the kitchen chair looking stricken.

"This is horrible," Robin said as she stared down at the table. "I'll never live up to this. I don't want to be the voice of my generation."

Angie and Barbara looked at her, shocked at this reaction.

Tracy put her hand on Robin's shoulder and spoke softly.

"Go get your jacket. Let's go out for a walk."

They headed down College Avenue away from campus toward Davis Square. The April weather was chilly and windblown. It had rained the night before and the streets were still wet. Robin zipped her old leather jacket up and stuffed her hands in her pockets. Tracy had on a navy blue pea coat with the collar turned up. She held onto Robin's arm as they walked.

"Where are we going?" Robin asked.

"I don't know. Let's see where we end up."

They walked past the small shops along Holland Street and passed Salsa Fresca, a Tex Mex restaurant with a white stucco exterior.

"Remember this restaurant?" said Robin.

"How could I forget? It was the first place we ate after we slept together two years ago."

"Yeah, I'm surprised they didn't throw us out. We couldn't keep our hands off each other."

Tracy smiled at her.

"I never want your hands off me, Robin. Not after two years and not after twenty."

Robin pulled Tracy to her.

"That's something you'll never have to worry about," she said and kissed Tracy.

229

They continued down a residential side street and found themselves on busy Massachusetts Avenue. Tracy peered across the wide expanse of four lanes with cars whizzing by at thirty miles an hour.

"Let's cross here."

Robin looked around her. There was nothing there but gas stations and non-descript buildings.

"Where are we going?"

"You'll see. It's not far."

There was a playground at the end of a block on a corner and Tracy guided them in through the gate in the chain link fence. The swings and slides looked almost brand new, all plastic in primary colors. There were no children on this cold day.

Tracy sat on a swing and motioned for Robin to sit next to her. They twisted their seats toward one another.

"You think you'll miss this place after we graduate? I mean Adams and, you know, Boston?" Tracy said.

"It'll always have meaning for me because it's where I met you, and Angie as well. But as long as the two of us are together I don't care where we are. I really mean that."

"You would have come back to Durham with me if I'd wanted that?"

Robin smiled.

"Kicking and screaming, but yes I would have. I noticed you didn't apply anywhere south of the Mason-Dixon Line."

"I wanted to be in New York with you. I think we can build a nice life there together."

Tracy dragged her feet along the dirt under the swing and wondered if she could push off and soar up high like she did when she was a little girl. They were quiet for a minute and then Tracy spoke up.

"Remember my conversation with Jeffy way back in the summer after freshman year when I told him about my feelings for you?"

"Yes, that was a major turning point in getting you to call me."

"It was," she said. "That day, I also told Jeffy that he needed to consider going to med school to become a psychiatrist. I told him that if he stayed in engineering, he'd be wasting his gift."

"Sounds like he listened to you. He was early accepted to the med school at Duke right?"

Tracy nodded, looked directly into Robin's eyes and reached for her hand.

"Honey, it's the same with you. You have a gift and I say that not to add more pressure, but because it's true. Don't worry about the review. Just keep working on that novel you've got going. The rest of it will take care of itself. I promise."

Robin got up from her swing and stood behind Tracy with her arms around her.

"I guess I can't go wrong if I listen to my muse, huh?"

She grabbed hold of the chains that attached the swing seat to the metal frame above and pulled Tracy toward her, letting go and watching her sail forward. As she swung back, Robin pushed again, this time with more force, and Tracy pumped her feet, going further upward in an arc off the ground. When Tracy returned, Robin pushed again and called out to her.

"C'mon baby let's see how high we can go."

Epilogue – 11 Years Later
Election Night, November 2008

"This is Chuck Jensen, WBTN Channel 9, Boston. We're gonna switch over now to Carlene Fowler at the Doubletree Hotel in Medford with the Antonelli for Congress campaign. Carlene, is Mayor Antonelli expected on stage soon for her victory speech?"

"Yes, Chuck, we've been told she's on her way down".

"Great crowd there tonight."

"Well, there's a lot for them to be celebrating. You know, Angie Antonelli came from behind in this race and pulled it out in just the last few weeks. So her supporters are very enthusiastic and maybe even a little bit relieved."

"Correct me if I'm wrong Carlene, but she's the first openly gay candidate to be elected to Congress in Massachusetts, right?"

"Well, yes, if we're talking about an initial race. As you know, Barney Frank has been repeatedly re-elected after he announced he was gay, but he did not initially run as an out of the closet candidate."

"There's a number of people up on the stage waiting for the Congresswoman-elect to arrive. Who do you recognize up there, Carlene?"

"Well, of course, we have the candidate's immediate and extended family; as you know they're a very political family. That's her mother, Jeannette, who has been the brains behind this campaign. And if we can get a shot over to the left, that's the writer, Robin Greene, a close friend that Mayor Antonelli met in college at Adams, if I'm not mistaken."

"Greene's novel won the Pulitzer last spring. The youngest author ever to do so. And who's that next to her?"

"That's her partner, Doctor Tracy Patterson, also a friend of Mayor Antonelli's from Adams. You know, Doctor Patterson specializes in working with creative types, like writers, who become stuck and have stopped writing."

"Does she turn them all into Robin Greenes?"

234

"I don't know Chuck, but you might want to pull that dusty old novel out of your drawer and make an appointment. Oh, here's the Mayor now coming up to the podium. Let's listen."

"Thank you, thank you all so much. Tonight the people of the Fifth District of our great Commonwealth of Massachusetts have sent a message to Congress, and that message is 'Stop the gridlock and get to work!' And you have my guarantee that I will get right to work and together we will make things happen for the hard working people of this district!"

(Cheers)

As Angie gave her victory speech, Robin took Tracy's hand. From their place on stage they could look out at the sea of faces in the cheering crowd. She caught a glimpse of her mother who had been living with the Antonellis for the last month, working full-time on the campaign. Patty Coolidge and her partner, Jenny, were also out there and she nudged Tracy to show her. Tracy then pointed to Charlie, who she still thought of as her fairy godmother, standing tall in his red beehive wig and a rather demure black and silver gown.

Marveling at the sight and entranced by the spectacle of it all, Robin turned to Tracy who was already looking at her.

"Did you ever think—"

Tracy cut her off.

"That we'd be standing right here one day? Yes, I did."

Robin smiled and nodded.

"Me too. Still, it's amazing that she won."

Tracy smiled and pointed to Robin. "And that you won."

"And you won too, Doctor Patterson."

235

Tracy squeezed Robin's hand.

"All three of us, here tonight, together after so many years. We all won."

###

THE AUTHOR

Cindy Rizzo lives in New York City with her partner, Jennifer, and the requisite two cats issued to every lesbian household (well, most). She has worked in philanthropy for many years and has a long history of involvement in the LGBT community, including membership on the founding board of Gay & Lesbian Advocates and Defenders (GLAD), the organization that first brought marriage equality to the US. In the 1970s and 1980s she wrote for Boston's *Gay Community News* and has published essays in the anthologies, *Lesbians Raising Sons* and *Homefronts: Controversies in Non-Traditional Parenting.* She was the co-editor of a fiction anthology, *All the Ways Home*, published in 1995 (New Victoria) in which her story "Herring Cove" was included. She serves on the boards of Congregation Beth Simchat Torah in New York and Funders for LGBT Issues. She is the mother, and her partner is the step-mother, of two grown sons and a wonderful daughter-in-law.

You can contact Cindy by email at cindyrizzobooks@gmail.com, via Facebook www.facebook.com/ctrizzo, through her blog, www.cindyrizzo.wordpress.com, or on Twitter @cindyrizzo.

ACKNOWLEDGEMENTS

The completion and publication of Exception to the Rule is
testament to the adage that "it takes a village." Here are the inhabitants of
mine.

First, the beta readers (go Team Beta!)—Donna MacArthur, Roz
Lee, Marie Esposito, Joann Lee and Nancy Heredia—who provided
incredibly helpful feedback on the first draft. Marie Esposito, an amazing
writer herself, gave me a lot of advice about the opening chapter, which led
to an important restructuring. Nancy Heredia has been my consigliere
throughout this entire process, and our growing friendship has been a
wonderful bonus.

Two editors helped with this book and both improved it greatly.
Nikki Busch was great to work with and to confide in along the way. She is
also the person responsible for suggesting the fabulous title of the book.
Jayne Fereday got me to the finish line with some additional feedback on
structure and the dreaded dialogue tags. Her help smoothed out some of
the remaining creases in the manuscript.

Kate Genet greatly improved my blurb and my brother-in-law, Jan
Wandrag, designed the amazing cover at a time when I was at my wits end
trying to figure out how this book should be visually represented. My
friend, Liz Scheier, who knows the world of e-books, gave me very helpful
advice over a couple of beers one night.

Along the way, it's been a surprise and delight to discover the lesfic
community and all of the incredible women who nurture and support the
growing body of lesbian fiction books. I've been enriched and greatly
assisted by the online lesfic community, especially those like Beni Gee,
Henriette Bookgeek, Mary Ann Frett and Jaynes Pehney, who ensure that

we remain connected to one another and that our work is celebrated and discussed.

I've also been so fortunate to be able to bend the ears of many other writers, some of whom have become good friends. A number of people provided really helpful and timely advice while I was in the throes of my deliberation about whether to publish indie or submit to a publisher. Their patience and generosity has inspired me to pay their gifts forward and be as helpful as possible to anyone who seeks me out.

I'd be horribly remiss if I didn't thank four of these writers by name. Joann Lee has been a wonderful support and I've so enjoyed our correspondence. Clare Ashton has been patient and helpful to me throughout all of my self-imposed drama about the cover and the blurb. Her own incredible writing makes me want to do better each time I look at a blank page and begin. Amy Dawson Robertson has acted as a mentor throughout this process, thoughtfully answering all of my questions and giving me so much of her time and the benefit of her experience. She has certainly earned the nickname "Awesome Dawson" and it was a great pleasure to sit for hours at dinner with her and her partner discussing books and writing and all manner of other things.

There aren't enough accolades to adequately thank my friend and a fabulous author, Kiki Archer, who has spent hours with me giving advice and being a cheerleader for this book. There's no one else I'd rather learn from about marketing and promotion. Hers has been the A-level class (I hope I got that reference to the British education system correct).

These writers have made a tremendous difference in my life. Please buy and read their books.

My partner, Jennifer Schwam, has been squarely in my corner throughout all of this. She listened to me read each page of this book, practically as it was being written. She was the one who introduced me to

Maslow's Hierarchy of Needs when I asked her what kind of psychology class would focus on human motivation. And she has been enormously patient with my periodic self-absorption and obsession about this book and all of the decisions I've had to make throughout the process. "I want to be kept in the loop," she's told me repeatedly. She has been and will always continue to be.

Finally, as odd as it might sound, I want to thank Robin, Tracy and Angie whose story began way back in 1990 when I started this book and who've waited patiently all these years for me to get on with it and finish writing about their college years. I have now, but I am far from done with them. And they with me.

Cindy Rizzo, November 2013

RESOURCES FOR HOMELESS LGBTQ YOUTH

Exception to the Rule deals, in part, with the issue of homelessness among LGBTQ youth. The fictitious organization, Boston Area Youth Services (BAYS), is a stand-in for many of the fine organizations in the US and the UK that support, serve and advocate for and with young people who've been driven from their homes. Here is a list of some of them:

The Albert Kennedy Trust
England, United Kingdom
www.akt.org.uk/

Lucie's Place
Little Rock, AR
www.luciesplace.org/

LA Gay & Lesbian Center
Los Angeles, CA
www.lagaycenter.org

Larkin Street Youth Services
San Francisco, CA
www.larkinstreetyouth.org

Zebra Coalition
Central Florida
www.zebrayouth.org

Home for Little Wanderers

Waltham House

Boston, MA

www.thehome.org

Youth on Fire

Cambridge, MA

www.aac.org/about/our-work/youth-on-fire.html

Ruth Ellis Center

Detroit, MI

www.ruthelliscenter.org

Bridge for Youth

Minneapolis, MN

www.bridgeforyouth.org

Ali Forney Center

New York, NY

www.aliforneycenter.org

FIERCE

New York, NY

www.fiercenyc.org

New Alternatives for LGBT Homeless Youth

New York, NY

www.newalternativesnyc.org

Sylvia's Place

New York, NY

www.mccnycharities.org/hys.html

LGBT Center of Raleigh

Raleigh, NC

www.lgbtcenterofraleigh.com

YouthCare

Seattle, WA

www.youthcare.org

CPSIA information can be obtained
at www.ICGtesting.com
Printed in the USA
LVOW01s1208130317
527020LV00005B/939/P